Invisible Things is a book about *devising*. Combining text, photographs, extracts from artist's notebooks, research notes, drawings and recorded dialogues, it presents a non-linear journey through a devising process, revealing all the complexities, explorations, changes of direction, strategies and discoveries that such an experience entails.

Written as a series of themed chapters intercut with case studies of elements of the process, *Invisible Things* is both evocative and specific, poetic and practical. The themed chapters cover subjects such as collaboration, dramaturgy and design; the case studies address things such as working with light, creating sound and music, approaching structure and organising rehearsals.

Invisible Things offers a rare chance to see the usually hidden activities that make up a devising process, by exploring that process from the point of view of the people at its heart.

GW00459143

A recording of **An Infinite Line: Brighton** can be viewed online at www.feveredsleep.co.uk/ aninfinitelinebrighton

INVISIBLE THINGS   *Documentation from a devising process*

This chapter presents some of the challenges of creating a performance that began as one person's research project and evolved into a large-scale event with many people in the creative and producing team. Touching on key moments, tensions, realisations and strategies, it evokes some of the joys and difficulties of collaborative practice.

23 09 06, 14:13

Being Alone, Becoming Many   [2–21]

Wednesday 12th April, 10.45am.
Leaving London. On the train.
Alone. Grey clouds: dark grey
through to white patches of
bright white, and hazy sky where
the sun's pushing through.
Meteorological chiaroscuro.
Spring: it's been sunny, raining,
warm, cold, snowing, all this week.
The changeability of spring.
    Approaching the ridge of the
South Downs. North side: cloud,
paler; whiter. Patches of blue sky.
Shadows and sun on the tops of
the hills. Into the tunnel: black.
Noise. Speed. Out of the tunnel:
more cloud; lower cloud. Still
white and grey (more grey);
still patches of blue sky.
    Approaching the city: the sky
brightens. Brightens; Brighton.
It begins like this. It has begun.

Extract from research diary kept
during a year of visits to Brighton
to look at the light

RESEARCH TASKS

1. A series of fixed places: a photograph taken. Repeat this every month. Record all times & positions.

2. Observation. Take notes. Write the experience

3. If the opportunity comes, ask, "what's the light like here in Brighton?"

4. Take a video. A panorama. Record all times & positions.

5. Watch the sun set - observation. Note. Describe. Evoke. Photograph. Record times & positions.

6. Watch the sun rise. Observe & record as above.

7. Answer the Question Set. Record all times & positions each time the questions are answered.

12 04 06, 15:02

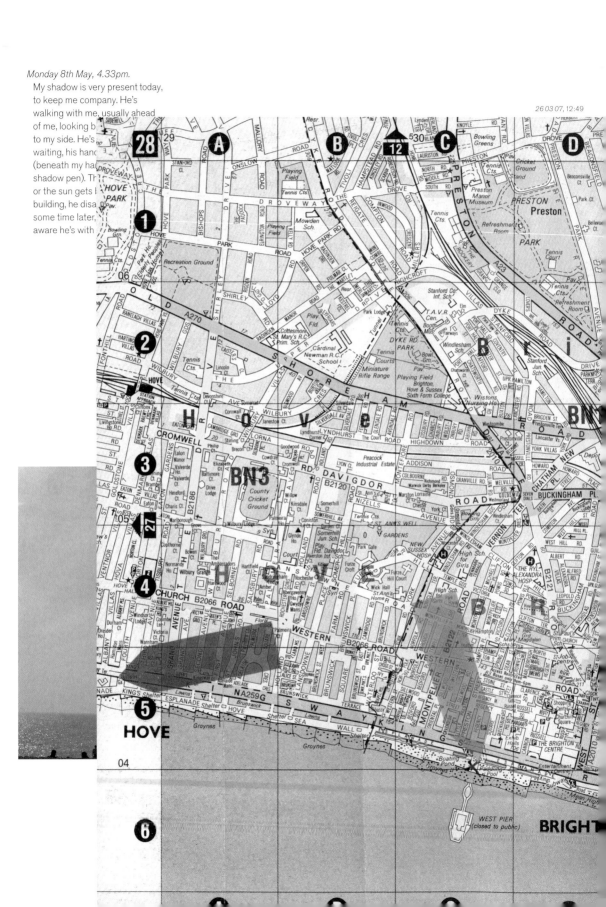

Monday 8th May, 4.33pm.
My shadow is very present today,
to keep me company. He's
walking with me, usually ahead
of me, looking b
to my side. He's
waiting, his hand
(beneath my ha
shadow pen). Th
or the sun gets
building, he disa
some time later,
aware he's with

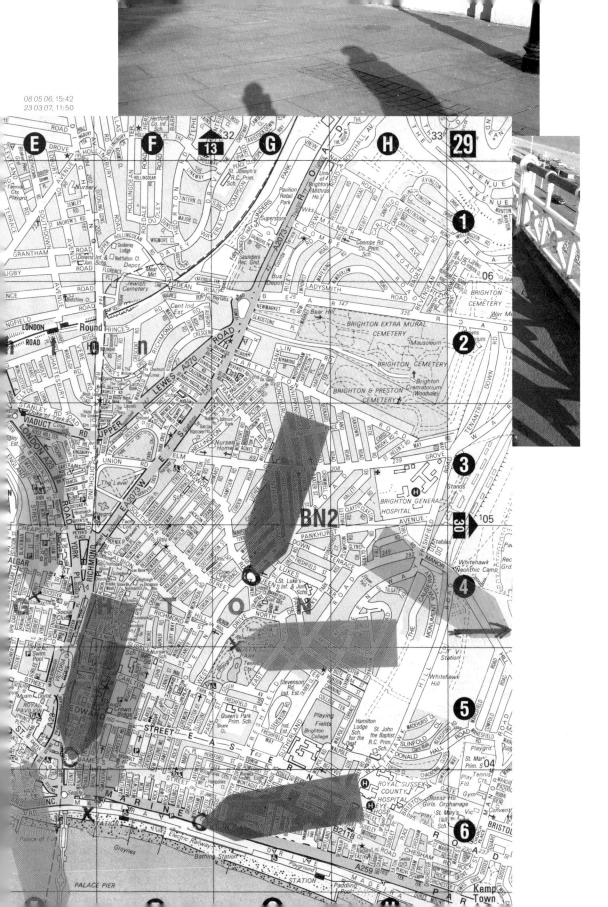

Before the project existed, before a title appeared, before a decision was made as to what to do, before any ideas, before the project turned from a possibility to an actuality, there was walking. There was walking and waiting. There was walking and waiting and looking and writing. There was a camera shutter, opening to the sky, blinking at the sea, taking in the city. There was a camera shutter in the body of a camera in the hand of a body in the landscape. There was my body in the weather: cold, wet, hot, squinty, warm, tired, bored, anxious, sad, excited, awed. All eyes: looking. Looking at the city, the sea, the sky, feeling the weather, searching out the light. There was loneliness and tiredness and confusion and revelation, persistence and walking and waiting and sitting on the beach, getting rained on, getting sunburned, getting damp as the mist rolled in, getting earache from the constant Westerly wind, drinking coffee and frowning as the light bounced back from a round metal pavement café table, dazzling, heavy legs, tired feet, waiting, happy. Waiting for a revelation, waiting for a release. There was a body here in the middle of the city, here on the hills to the East, here in the sea-salt scour at the end of the pier in the middle of winter; running East, walking North; here in this park, surrounded by green, beneath a blue sky, haze hovering, a curtain, a veil, a screen; here on the beach waiting and watching and writing as the sun refuses to set.

It began like this: I am alone, travelling to Brighton (alone except most times in the company of a dog). I am alone walking from the station to a B&B. I am alone as I rise to greet the morning sun; as I wait for the sun to set. I am alone as I wander the hills behind Roedean School, alone in the narrow streets, in the middle of the city, in the crowd, on the flesh-filled beach. But not alone: here with the city to shelter me, with the sea to hold me, with the sky to look over me, with the clouds, the weather. Here with the light.

For a year I travel to Brighton, alone, to walk, to wait, to look, to try to see, to try to understand what makes the light here like it is. A visit each month, for a day or two or three. Pure research. I travel with a set of questions, and a task, a set of instructions for me to follow, to guide me on my journey with the light. I write. Ideas for a project come and go. I write proposals for the Festival, I change my mind, some ideas solidify, some disperse. Many more ideas are discarded than are carried forward:

generate too much then delete, cut, edit, change. The pleasure of
imagination and invention. Too many ideas, so I decide to make a project
in three parts: a book, an installation and a performance, each in its own
way a response to the light. The performance will be complex, site specific:
it will contain performers, live music, a space filled with objects and sound,
all kinds of lighting ideas, and the possibility of working with an animal.
If I want to make this happen, it makes sense for the project to be made by
Fevered Sleep, to have that support, that framework (I have always made
work independently from Fevered Sleep as well as with the company:
double opportunities, double the chance of finding money, finding
resources, double the chance of making the making of the work possible).
But this project feels big. I don't want to make it alone.

    And so I am no longer alone.

As things become clearer, the number of people around the
project changes.

1   Just me (my visits, my walking, my writing, my ideas).
2   Me and Ghislaine (we work with the festival to try to make
    it happen).
3   Me and Ghislaine and Jane (we talk about possibilities and timing,
    try to pin something down).
4   Me and Ali and Sophie and Louise (we have a date. 2008:
    it will happen).
6   Me and Ali and Sophie and Louise and Kevin and Cindy (talking
    about a horse).
16   Me and Ali and Jo and Synne and Sam and Laura and Joseph and
    Jamie and David and Jamie and Mark and Sophie and Louise and
    Kevin and Cindy and a horse (initial R&D).
14   Me and Ali and Jo; and me and Synne and Laura and Jamie and
    Jamie and David and Mark and Ruth and Cathy and Robin and
    Delphine and Douglas (developing design ideas; R&D focused on
    working with the notes from my research visits).
21+   Me and Ali and Jo and Synne and Sam and Laura and Jamie and
    David and Jamie and Mark and Beth and Billy and Sophie and

Louise and Sharon and Matt and Jane and Tanya and press and
interviews and photographers and Kevin and Cindy and a horse
(devising, rehearsals, prep.).
80+ And an audience.

From a body alone in the cold wet warm dry hot still squinty wind-blown
foggy landscape to a company all here in The Basement, with an audience,
eighty bodies together in the dark, still looking, still waiting, still trying to
understand, still trying to see.

An Infinite Line: Brighton was a strange project: on the one hand it was a
collective endeavour, its creation the shared responsibility of a team;
on the other it was an act of auteurship, the result of one person's vision.
It was *our* project, but to begin with, and probably in the end, it was *mine*,
and even in that room full of other people, I could never stop feeling like
I was in it alone.

I remember:
How we struggled to work out what to do with the notes from my research.
After the first period of R&D it became clear that we wanted to work with
the notes as part of the performance, as a text, a script of sorts, but we
didn't know how to. The notes were never written to be spoken, only as
a way of recording an experience. How would we translate this into
performance? How do we perform an unperformable set of notes, twenty
thousand words, repetitive, circular, dense? Whose voice is it that speaks
these notes, my notes? Where is the speaking body? Is it just here, in this
basement, reading these words? Is it in the theatrical frame, 'acting',
recreating the experience of being there on the beach, walking through
the city, waiting for the light? We conducted many experiments around
this, explored the notes being read from paper; spoken verbatim from a
recording listened to through headphones; pre-recorded and played back
like a voiceover; read straight and processed and translated from words
to music to dance to image to sound. One voice becoming many voices,
one form becoming many forms.

*How it became clear that this process for the rest of the creative team –
of trying to make sense of the notes – was parallel to my own experience
of trying to make sense of the light.*
In many ways, the collaborative devising process was a mirror to my
research process. Where I had started with no understanding of the
particularity of Brighton's light, and the year of visits had been about trying
to find a way to see and feel and understand it, we started to work together
with no idea – I soon realised I had no idea – how to translate that
experience into a performance event full of other things, not only the light,
not only the notes, not only my experience. The notes from my research
visits began as a means to record an experience, but grew from this to a
form of textual memory that emerged as poetry. They expressed my
attempts to find a way of translating natural light into another form, into
words. This idea – the importance of the attempt itself – became a way in
for us: the performance would be a place in which we all could *try to find
a way* to translate the experience of the light into a live experience, into
an event. This collective striving, our struggle to understand what we were
doing there, in that basement, in the dark, became our guiding principle.

How I often felt confused as to why there were so many people in the room.
On the first day of R&D in August 2007 I wrote "What are they doing here?"
in my notebook. I didn't know what to do with all these bodies, when I had
been so used to my body being in the project alone. I remember thinking
that there might be one person who does nothing but speak; *one* person
who never stops moving; the ensemble reduced to a collection of
individuals, somehow separate at the same time as working together
through the piece. There was a conflict of sorts embedded in the very
decision to create this performance in the form I chose. The set was
flexible, and could be reconfigured and moved around the space, but this
took more than one person to do. The presence of a horse meant his trainer
was always on stage, and it meant that everyone else onstage had to be
aware of where he was, or move him, or move around him. The ways we
had explored ideas in the R&D had such a strong reliance on ideas of
translation (e.g. a sunset becoming a cine film becoming a source of light
used to light someone as they danced, and the dance used as a score for

a music improvisation) that very little of the material had any sense of solitude: we were making an ensemble performance, we were all in it together. My job became one of working out what to do with each of the people I had invited into the project, and to work out how to bring them, and my earlier experience, together.

How we worked together during devising periods.
We would meet, we would warm up: stretch, do yoga, skip, play games. We would do a lot of work with rhythm, complex rhythmic physical exercises, to get our different bodies moving together, being together, developing a sense of each other. I was insistent that everyone joined in this, including those people who didn't want to. The performers did more physical and musical warming up – they needed to – but everyone played the games. The games were markers in the rhythm of our day: after warm up, after dinner, whenever we got stuck.

How important improvisation was.
It became vital to create a space in which each person in the team was able to explore ideas, test possibilities, make suggestions. We had the luxury of a lot of R&D, in phases that gave us opportunities to focus on different things at different times. I asked a lot of questions, prompts to give a frame-work for the others' play. We invited other people to step temporarily into the process, bringing new points of view, to see what fresh possibilities might open up. Improvisation led to ownership: a sense that *we* were making this material that was growing out of an experience *I* had had.

How the project became part of our lives.
We all moved to Brighton for two months for rehearsals and for the Festival. We stayed together in various combinations, visiting each other's flats, seeing who had the best view (not me), feeding each other, drinking together, going to the beach together. David brought his family to Brighton so they could be together. Work like this is hard to separate from all the other complexities of getting on with living. For me, a project is a cuckoo: it supplants and displaces, pushes away the other elements of life, aggressive in its will to survive.

How we formed smaller groups and micro-communities within the
larger company.
These smaller groupings gave all of us strategies for coping, frameworks
for talking and supporting each other and working together. They drifted
across other constellations that were to do with who lived together, who
spent time with whom, who had worked with me before, who was new.
Half of us had come straight from making another project together; other
people joined us just for *An Infinite Line: Brighton*. I would spend a lot of
time with Ali, telling her like no-one else how I was feeling about the work.
I spent a lot of time with Ali and Jo, talking design. With Synne, talking
about ideas, about structures, about strategies. With Mark, cutting up cine
film, making moving light. Jamie and David and Mark necessarily talked a
lot about sound. We organised various meetings, different people coming
to each. We made sure there were moments when we all came together just
to talk, to reflect, to take stock. This was built into our working day, but of
course the talking and the gathering and the making-continuing-possible
bled out around our schedule. Laura and Jamie and Mark formed a semi-
secret DVD-watching club (I think it was semi-secret; I still don't really
know if it actually existed or not). I remember us all on the Waltzers on
the pier together at night, feeling sick, laughing. I remember standing in
the street with Sam just before starting an afternoon session, crying.
The transition from one to many was difficult.

I remember this:
We spent a long time creating frameworks for improvisations, endlessly
playing, trying things out, testing ideas. We invented different categories of
material: 'poetic images', 'the text as the event', 'moments of taking stock',
'atmospheres', 'specific and tiny things', 'too-big things'. At the beginning
of the second week of rehearsals, less than three weeks before first night,
we ran a long improvisation to test an idea that the performance itself would
be largely improvised. I thought we would shift between these categories
in a free and endlessly changing way: that this fluidity and this movement
would be the essence of the event. I was fairly sure this was how we would
work. We ran the improvisation. It didn't work. I remembered all the things
I had imagined the project might be. I remembered the joy, the intensity,

the pleasure of being alone with the light. The improvisation didn't feel like anything I had imagined. Later, I called that day Black Monday. It was another pivot. Do we spend the rest of the rehearsal period working on ways of making it possible to have this always-improvised structure, or do we change direction, make a piece which is more structured, directed; still with a sense of fluidity, a sense of changeability, but ultimately more directed by me? A combination of fear, pressure, confusion. A sense of clarity about one thing at least: that improvisation hadn't worked. Not because of any flaw in any of the team, but because we hadn't worked long enough to make it possible for all these different people to hold all these different ideas up simultaneously and keep them in balance, keep them alive, keep them working. So I turned us in a different direction. With very little time we turned from that idea of a performance that would be improvised, to an idea of a performance we had to structure, that was more fixed. And we didn't have enough time – I didn't have enough time – to do that.

Searching for this structure, I remember feeling lost. I remember thinking, "What do they want me to say?" I remember waiting for a moment of clarity, waiting for something we did to feel right, waiting to regain my equilibrium so that I could actually work, waiting for inspiration. I remember waiting for the audience, wanting that closure on the waiting, but not wanting them to come. A note I had written during a research visit in May 2006 became a guide, and a key phrase in the performance: "I feel tired. Like I'm searching for something I only find if I invent it for myself." To search for something that doesn't yet exist, to know you're searching for it, and to not yet know what it is: that is devising.

This sounds bleak. I also remember thinking the material we made was exquisite, *exactly* what I had always hoped and imagined it would be. I remember how much I loved the people I was working with, how humbled I felt that they would spend two months in a dark basement, trying to respond to my experience of the light. The material was strong: the structure was the problem. We found a way through, pieced things together step by step. Try ideas, assemble things to see how they feel together, disassemble them, try them differently, cut, move, alter, try again. We knew, I knew, we had set ourselves an almost impossible task. But we had to try. I had to try.

The 'I' that sat on the hilltop in 2006, looking down over the city to the sea, was not the same 'I' that sat in The Basement, looking down at a tabletop covered in notes on material we had created, moving things around, trying to make sense of a bewildering array of fragmented stuff. The 'I' that had experienced a deliriously pleasurable research process was not the same 'I' that rehearsed exhausted after another sleepless night. The 'we' that first met during the R&D, when all we did was play and carelessly create, and the 'we' that presented to an audience was not the same 'we'. The individual and the group change through time and as soon as one becomes more than one, each person has to become a different person in order for work and exchange to be possible. Identity is complex, multiple, and each day there was a different group of people in the room, with different desires, different feelings, different ideas. The time we spent changed us; the process changed us; the light changed us; the weather changed us; the audience changed us. The project changed us.

Devising is a journey, from past to present, from memory to event, from there to here.

I remember this:
The performance started with Jamie and Laura listening, through head-phones, to a recording of the notes from my research visits: listening to my voice repeating that experience. They repeated those words for the audience. The performance ended with Jamie using an old tape player to record Laura as she described a September sunset, and then everyone listening to that recording playing back, as Laura danced, and then as a hard white light flooded the space.
    A journey, from my voice to Laura's voice.
    From my experience to their experience.
    From being alone to being many.
    And all of us being alone and becoming one of many, attempting to make sense of the light.

back from NICE

Installation

at Alexandra Place
Artists Brainstorm @ RCA

Installation

Installation

poster set

| T | F | S | S | M | T | W | T | F | S | S | M | T | W |
|1|2|3|4|5|6|7|8|9|10|11|12|13|14|

4   ROLL INVOICE

LIVERPOOL
Gail 11.45
Green Mellish 12 - 2.30
  Associates
Elizabeth Nellis - cl. 1R Care
6.15 o.k. p.t.l.

-6 Rehearse

3.o

rythe / Dance Umbrella

LENCA 5/3

IGHTON

pm meet Jane

IGHTON 12pm meet
        Sophie
        (in that bar)

day

(→10) Physio

Doctor

Installation   thursday 15

Ray

              cartan   friday 16

Installation

sheffield?
BRIGHTON LIGHT   saturday 17

                        Parking

Father's Day (UK & 2 of Ireland) sunday 18

| T | F | S | S | M | T | W | T | F | S | S | M | T | W |
|15|16|17|18|19|20|21|22|23|24|25|26|27|28|29|30|

10/2.30   thursday 12

BRIGHTON
LIGHT

10/1.30   friday 13

SHOPPING

11/2
BAC FIT UP 9-12 LGT   saturday 14
project   PARTICIPANTS 1-8
11/2   sunday 15
(ARTICIPANTS 1 →)
(TRART 5 →)

| S | M | T | W | T | F | S | S | M | T | W | T | F | S |
|15|16|17|18|19|20|21|22|23|24|25|26|27|28|29|30|31|

St. David's Day (PSM calling) thursday 1

LAURA 11am LL pt Rehearsal

4pm Lunch, Smills LB

SD Studio talk

                     friday 2

1pm physio   saturday 3

                     sunday 4

The Lord's Day

Tim's Dary

| T | F | S | S | M | T | W | T | F | S | S | M | T | W |
|1|2|3|4|5|6|7|8|9|10|11|12|13|14|

17 monday   Cal → Sue Emms

Camille in concert

18 tuesday 9 Doug / Antigon VIDEO

2 - 3 pm TSTT C → mutra
(Vicky skiing show)

19 wednesday

BRIGHTON LIGHT

JULY
WEEK 29   7K9LN9FiG
(Tour 8 - week off?)

6 monday Warwick 1st immedit
121   Advert
*61*121*10*0#
           n= of seconds

7 tuesday 10 —1 meet Annie & LAC

Rehearse 2-6

8 wednesday   RKI on the
10   show at 1.30
                 (to London)
1   POLKA EVENT
                 (ends 4.30)

NOVEMBER W T F S S M T W T F S S
WEEK 45   1 2 3 4 5 6 7 8 9 10 11 12

LENCA 5/3

26 monday

BRIGHTON VISIT

                     Parkins

27 tuesday

7pm → Camera Lighting /
      large meeting at BAC

28 wednesday 9.15 clean

11.30 meet Joey Deadline for RAE
1.30 physio
2.30 meet Tina

9.15

MARCH   T F S S M T W T F S S M T W
WEEK 13 1 2 3 4 5 6 7 8 9 10 11 12 13 14

Brighton LiGHT

3pm meet Jane

                     friday 21

No Ready to place Summer Submission

KLUB KALI
(Sean → London Subram) ? saturday 22

                     sunday 23

| M | T | W | T | F | S | S | M | T | W | T | F | S | S |
|15|16|17|18|19|20|21|22|23|24|25|26|27|28|29|30|31|

10/1   x Rydal AM   thursday 9
Heri Theatre at Polke, 1.30 p

Rebecca Belden
Voxybox   if S with
13/11 Ted christ - immedit
10/1 10am Angel Thea 10 Hm no
(Glwne 1.15pm cl)   ch
meet with Lois, Jo, Ged 2 - 6
                          RAC
*X 21 * (number)#(Green)
to set client to answer
11/2 phone number saturday 11
          2
BRIGHTON LIGHT
Remembrance Sunday sunday 12

| W | T | F | S | S | M | T | W | T | F | S | S | M | T |
|15|16|17|18|19|20|21|22|23|24|25|26|27|28|29|30|

9.15 302341584 train nt

DESIGN / PRODUCTION DAY WITH ALI from 9.30
1 DAY in Brighton 12-4 feb TV
2 DAY in Belfast
                   until 6
9.15   thursday 29

9am physio   friday 30
FS DAY 10.15 →
        1pm meet Shauna

SD studio in space   BRIGHT saturday 31
KX 4.45 → X-k   to nights chow

                     sunday 1

| T | F | S | S | M | T | W | T | F | S | S | M | T | W | T | F | S |
|15|16|17|18|19|20|21|22|23|24|25|26|27|28|29|30|31|

17

7. Answer the Question Set

What colour is the city?

What colour is the sky?

What colour is the sea?

What is the texture of the light?

What is the sound of the light?

How do I feel?

What's the weather like?

Where is the light now, where do I notice it, now?

26 08 06, 16:49
12 10 06, 17:52

26 08 06, 11:17

12 10 06, 16:32

Wednesday 20th July, 12.44am.
The sea: black. The sky: black.
The garland lights of the sea front
set against an infinite black void
beyond. Infinite absence, abyss,
light's lack and limit.

19 07 06, 23:52

Postscript (a note on risk)

Writing and rereading this chapter, I remember again how difficult it was to move through the final phases of the project, how overwhelming it felt, how terrifying. The project seems to me, now, to have been built on foundations of risk: the risks associated with an ambitious design on a very tight budget; the risks in deciding to work with a horse; the risks attached to the change in direction with the structure; the personal risk of opening up a private experience to other people, and of revealing that process to an audience. Each of these things brought its own problems and its own agonising. Each could have been the block on which the project stumbled.

Looking back, now, I remember *An Infinite Line: Brighton* as a piece that revealed itself through a process characterised by the unexpected. Although it was a piece that, in the end, I loved, it was not the piece I'd imagined, and I found it the most difficult piece to watch: every night my heart in my throat, stomach knotted, not knowing whether this time it would be a good performance, or one where the meeting of the audience and the performers and the material was misaligned.

To devise is to take a risk, of course, especially when the conditions of production are necessarily defined by limited time and money. To enter a space with nothing and to conjure something, even with the benefit and the luxury of a lot of R&D: there is always a danger there, a danger of failing to find the thing you hope to find; of failing to find a place in which you can meet with the other people you're working with, or with the audience; a danger that the desires and dreams you wrap around your ideas prove to be hollow, wasted, lost.

Dreams and desires start each process; risks and dangers threaten it. Out of that conflict, the work appears, and its emergence is always painful and always fraught, at the same time as being a narrative of pleasure, as surprising as a gift.

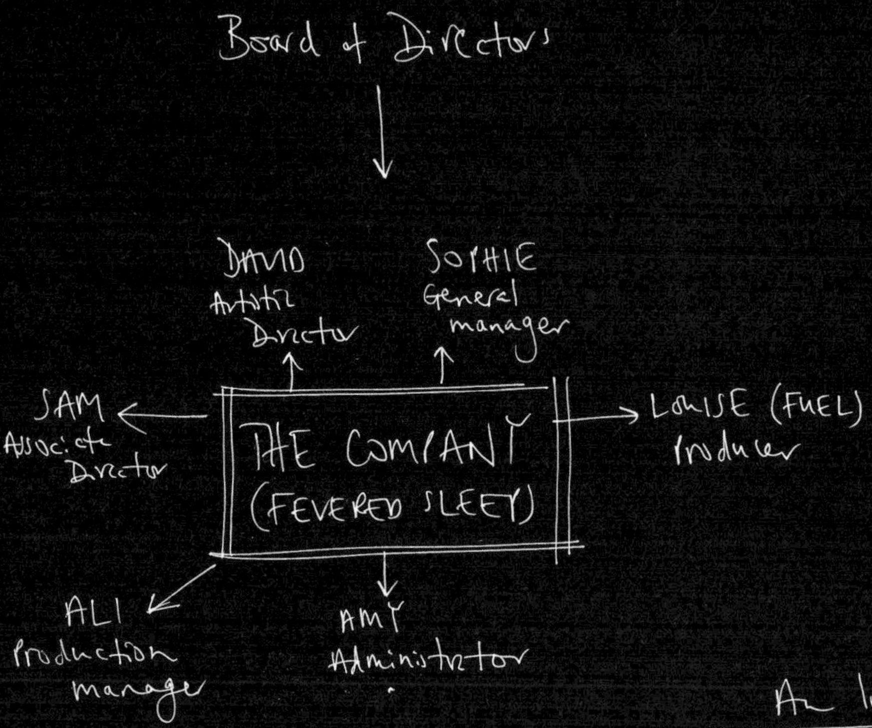

Board of Directors

↓

DAVID
Artistic
Director

SOPHIE
General
manager

SAM ←
Associate
Director

THE COMPANY
(FEVERED SLEEP)

→ LOUISE (FUEL)
Producer

ALI ↙
Production
manage

AMY
Administrator

An Infinite Line

... PEOPLE

Who made the making of An Infinite Line: Brighton possible?

The overall team can be broken down into five smaller groupings:

> **The company:** the people who provide the framework for how Fevered Sleep operates.

> **The creative team:** the artists, performers, creators, designers.

> **The producing/management team:** the people who looked after the finances, the marketing, who liaised with the Festival and managed all our relationships with the venue, funders, press.

> **The production team (different from the producing team):** the people who made the technicalities of the project hold together.

> **The incomers:** all those people, from within the producing team and from elsewhere, who stepped in and out of the creative process. The brevity of their involvement was the thing that was useful – providing a different point of view on emerging ideas and material.

In different ways each person in the project brought to it a quality or an energy or a practical process that made it possible for us to work together in the way that we did, and to create the material that we created. With hindsight, it's possible to name these different functions and roles in a way that reveals why they were important to the project: the sources, the confidantes, the enablers, the interrupters, the provocateurs, the illuminators, the eyes, the compasses (see overleaf).

Why choose to work in this particular way, with people assuming these kinds of roles? This structure for a group of people gathered around a project was unique to *An Infinite Line: Brighton*, and other projects have other groups of people who work in these ways, or more often in different ones. One consistent thing is that we don't work with set designers or scenographers, but evolve scenographic elements as part of a wider devising process, with direction and devising and design being intertwined. Making image-led work, it has always felt impossible to think about opening up the responsibility for creating a design to someone with a designated title, 'designer'. The set elements for *An Infinite Line: Brighton* were created by me, Ali and Jo, and emerged gradually as an organic part of the process of thinking about everything else. Once design ideas became more concrete, Ali would solve the technical problems of how to make them materialise physically, and was responsible for technical drawings and for liaising with the set builders and makers to whom we would contract out the construction work.

Starting out on a new project, we never sit down and say, "OK, who will the enablers be? Who are the interrupters, who are our confidantes?" – categories that I can now see were important for the realisation of this piece were not ones we self-consciously constructed. What these groupings reveal is how the people working together on a project must bring combinations of creativity, pragmatics, rigorousness, honesty and support. Through these different things we all pushed against each other and against the material, we all supported each other and the material, we all gave what needed to be given to each other and to the material, and it was through that friction and that cushioning and that giving that it was possible for the piece itself to emerge.

R+D collaborators

ALi + Jo (Design) ← SOURCES → Mar

performers   musicians

The Sources: The people who brought or generated ideas.

The Eyes: The people who were separate from the actual processes of creation, and who were literally or metaphorically 'set back' from the work, and therefore able to see it from a point of view that was different from mine (the idea of people seeing the work with 'fresh eyes' – i.e. as an audience member would, with no knowledge of the processes we had gone through to make something – was especially important).

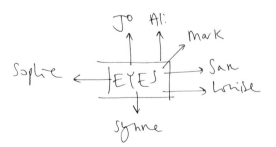

Jo Ali

Sophie ← EYES → Mark
                → San
                → Louise

Synne

The Provocateurs: The people who, during the devising process itself, would ask me questions about what was happening in the work, and why; or who would give feedback on what they were seeing and offer criticism of things that they thought were effective or unsuccessful in the context of the piece.

The Interrupters: The people who know you well enough and who you trust enough to be able to come in at any point and say, "That doesn't work", and who are removed enough from the process for that question to pre-empt the audience's arrival and their response.

[INTERRUPTERS]
↓
Sam

[COMPASSES] → Sophie
↓
Louise

The Compasses: The people who helped me to keep on track, who brought reassurance and who reminded me why we were there (I remember saying to Louise, "Don't let me make a theatre piece" when I was struggling to work out the structure and started to lose sight of what I wanted to do with the material, and she consistently encouraged me to take risks, to follow my instinct. I remember all the times when Sophie came in from the office, or when we were chatting during breaks, and she would say, "We can do this; you can do this": making it possible to believe we would find something which we wanted to show).

The Confidantes: The people who you need to be able to talk to, reveal your inner feelings to, have a moan to when you need to get something off your chest, especially if you feel that it's not appropriate to reveal these things in the context of the rehearsal room; people who you know are able to hear the things you need to say without it knocking them off balance.

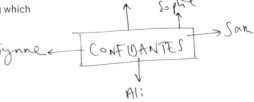

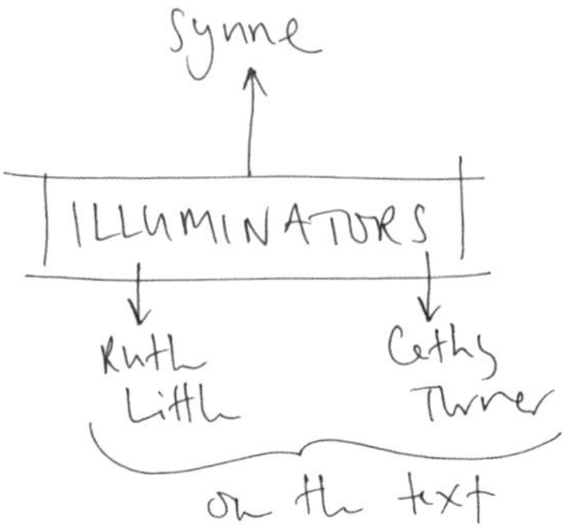

The Illuminators: The people who help you see things you hadn't noticed in the material, who share ideas with you in ways that bring revelations and discoveries; whose observations allow you to observe things from a different point of view. This happened during the R&D when we were working with different people who joined us to look at a specific thing (text, movement, direction), and it was the key aspect of the relationship between director and dramaturg in the project.

The Enablers: The people who look after the practicalities and pragmatics, who make it possible for the creative process to happen.

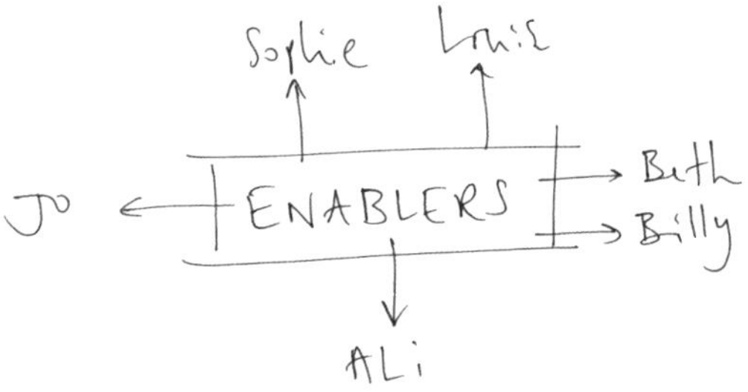

Synne

↑

| ILLUMINATORS |

Ruth Little   Cathy Turner

on the text

Sophie   Louis

↑   ↑

Jo ← | ENABLERS | → Beth
                      → Billy

↓

ALi

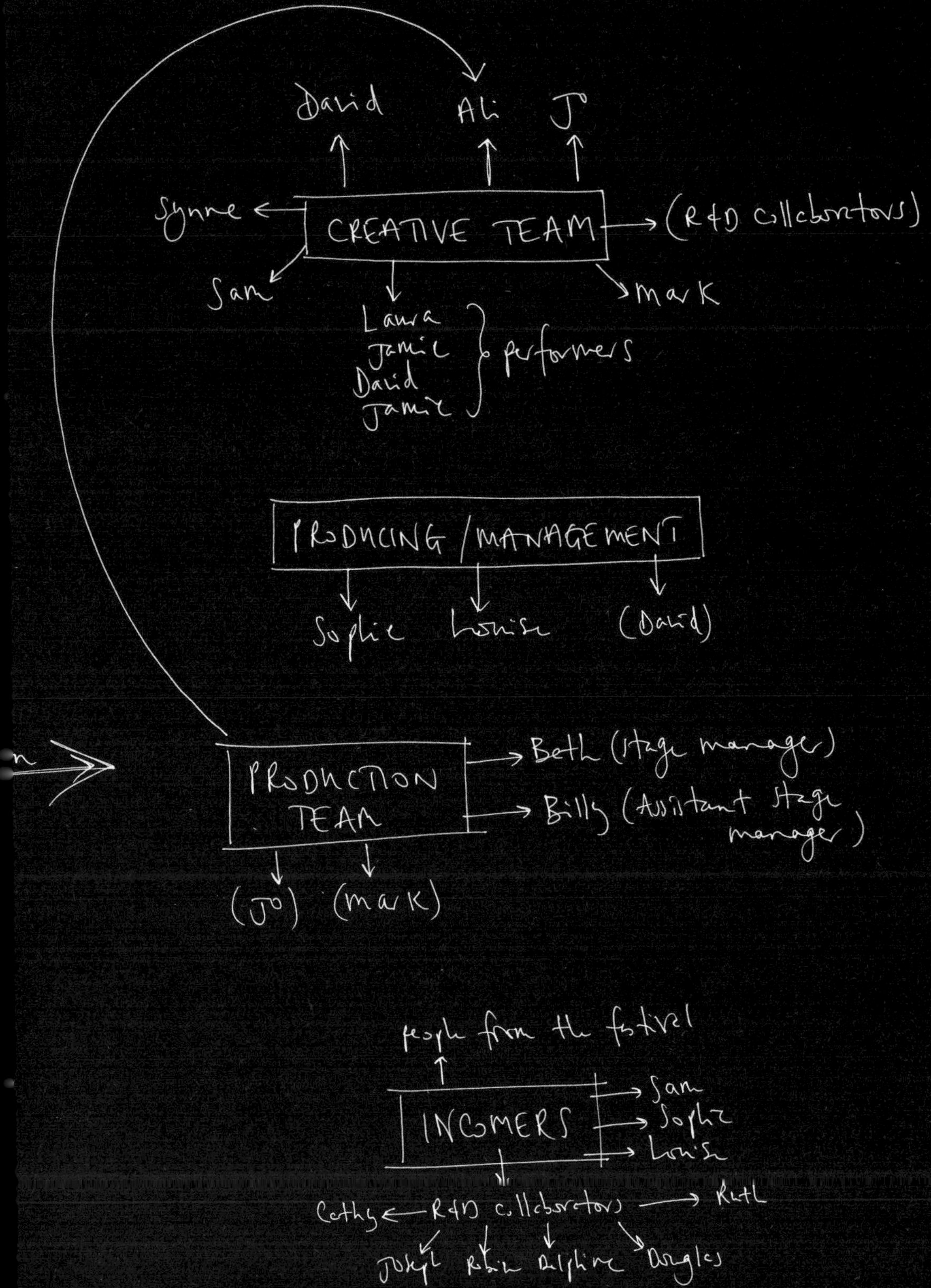

David   Ali   Jo

Synne ← CREATIVE TEAM → (R+D collaborators)

Sam

Mark

Laura
Jamie
David   } performers
Jamie

PRODUCING / MANAGEMENT

Sophie   Louise   (David)

PRODUCTION TEAM → Beth (stage manager)
→ Billy (Assistant stage manager)

(Jo) (Mark)

people from the festival

INCOMERS → Sam
→ Sophie
→ Louise

Cathy ← R+D collaborators → Ruth

Joseph Robin Delphine Douglas

Monday 26th March, 10.10am.
There's something about space,
something about the streets
repeatedly opening up to a view
of sky and sea, t
distance, air, ligh
And something
and dip of hills, c
the city, streets
living map.
   There's somet
sea, of course, a
variable slab of c
and light, a mirrc
light, reflector, e
perpetual, infinit
and change.
   There's somet
Downs, about th
system of air an
create, and som
chalk, brownwhi
paleness of the
   There's somet
city's orientatior
sea, and the per
streets and view
   There's somet
Westerly wind, e
lids narrowed ag
and the light.
   And there's sc
the city, about th
buildings, about
the yellow and tl

This chapter explores the significance of the visual in the project, and reflects
on some of the ways in which the urban and natural landscapes of Brighton –
and its light – were translated into performance images. Structured as a
series of visual essays, it presents ideas to do with mirrors and reflection;
with frames, architectural perspectives and the performance site; with the
presence of a single sun-like source of light; with colour; and with the
significance of chalk. Each of these visual essays – which, as in other
chapters, enfold a written essay reflecting further on light, design and space
– maps phases of research, observation, translation, experimentation and
presentation: microcosms of the processes that were at the heart of every
aspect of making the piece.

12 11 06, 09:57

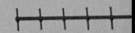

Light, Design, Space   [28–79]

There's something about space, something about the
a view of sky and sea, to a view of spa
(spread). And something about the coast and
the city, streets laid out like a living map

There's something about the sea, of course, about
slabs of color, movement and light, a mi
emitter, absorber, reptacle, infinite movement a

There's something about the towns, about the se
weather they create, and something about
(greatness) of the surrounding hills.

There's something about the city! one future
and the perpendicularity of streets

There's something about that wintery wind, ey
against the cold and the light.

And there's something about the city, about the
about the cream of the yellow of the wh

repeatedly opening up to
once, air, light, of
hills, of those vistas t

i infinitely variable
a source of light, reflects,
ange.

vister of air and
anmulite, about the

and they
flick back.

ting, lots narrowed

12 11 06, 09:58

buildings

Wednesday 12th April, 4pm.
Gardner Street. Blinding light
bouncing off the outdoor metal
table. Dulled when the sun
goes behind a c
around here: sur
sunglasses on, s
sunglasses off..

…

Saturday 26th Au
The back end of
still hot. Behind
low, thin and hea
sun's still brillian
and white. Wher
through, the daz
harsh, burning b
There are the
clouds of summ
out of season: b
massive light be
Summer clouc
sun breaks throi
transformed: the
dull flat metal to
mirror made of r
The colours quix
infinitely, rapidly
now a uniform g
streak of silver, r
metal, now brigh
now a heavy pla
wheeling sky.
Summer is ch
Grey but blindin
warm, sun but cl
And still, wher
check, a differer

…

Thursday 12th Oc
From here, high
spread out, flat-l
edge of the sea.
vista of brown ai
So much whit
Reflective. A r
by the reflective
sea, hemmed in,
these hills.

…

Tuesday 27th Ma
To the South, the
liquid mirror, daz
light like a magr
same pole with i
to the North, the
earthy reflection
back the other v

MIRRORS / REFLECTION

Why *is* the light in Brighton so particular? Is it the odd microclimate that is created by the landmass of the Downs cutting off the city from the country behind it? Is it the mass of water acting as a huge mirror for the sky and the light? Is it the mist, the rain, the fog, that hang around the coast? Is it the combination of the blackness out over the water, and the brilliance of the edge of the city? Is it what I see, or what I think, or what I feel?

From second project proposal for Brighton Festival, November 2005

20 01 07, 15:03

[32]

12 11 06, 10:11
29 09 06, 17:02

24 09 06, 10:00

what is the
texture
of ligLt ?

Brighton: tiles,
shingles,
of reflectivity,
of mirror,
overlapping like scales.

Tiles.

Shimmer,
flutter,
flicker in the wind.

A mirrored surface, reflecting light,
harsh, metallic, liquidsilver:

The mirror tiles

Water on the floor, a pool, a puddle

Mylar – a metallic foil – laid out
on the floor.

Not about the light but an evocation
of the light.

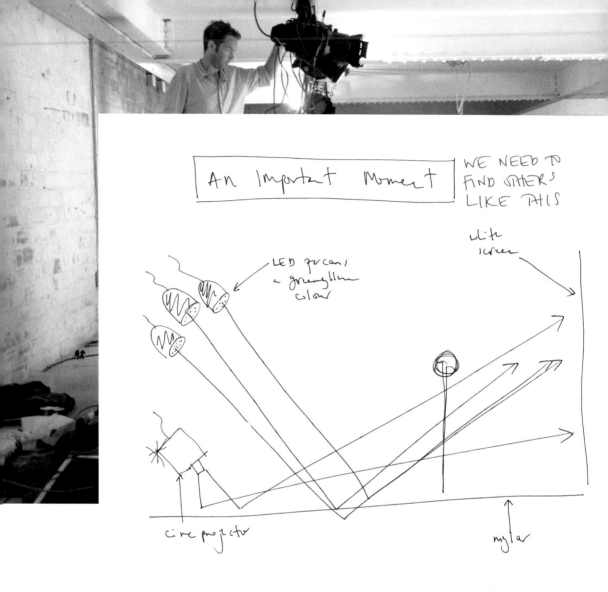

An Important Moment | WE NEED TO FIND OTHERS LIKE THIS

LED p3 cans
a green yellow
colour

white
screen

cine projector

mylar

The combination of the aqua light colour
and the songild projection, and the
colour quality of the silhouette/shadow
bounced up onto the screen: for the first
time we create an image that looks
like an image from others: an
accurate recreation: blueblack silhouetted
bodies against a shimmering golden sea

Again, this effort of creating an image, of attempting to achieve something significant. I love this, that the performers so visibly expose their effort to achieve this significance, this relevance. This is really important to the idea of the task being impossible.

(pp.38–9)
Something's Approaching,
An Infinite Line: Brighton,
the performance, May 2008

Sunday 21st January, 11.15am.

The sky is filmic.

That Western wind blows clouds
fast across the frame (the screen)
of this street.

The picture: a
sea, moving Eas
blue brown whit
through the sky.
diorama, of sky a

A compass cit
Walking West
Advocaat sun

Look East at t
blue sky

Look South: s
framed sea

North: the city
not light.

The buildings
the sky. Brown,
blue frame: and
there, through tl
to the left, or the
fragments of the
but each fragme
cloudless duck e
left; grey blue be
greywhite cloud
watery greyblue
stripe of fragile
The sky in this
the skies in this
each frame hold
each sky a diffe
picture a differe
time I look.

FRAMES / ARCHITECTURAL PERSPECTIVES / THE SITE

This idea grows out of my experience of walking around the city, catching glimpses of the sea, being aware of the different light above me, around me, down streets and against buildings: it's a flâneur's project [...] and there'll be a space, probably a big space, an open space, a space that can accommodate something as big as the light.

From third project proposal for Brighton Festival, March 2006

28 03 07, 12:02

23 09 06, 16:13

08 05 06, 16:28

09 05 06, 13:55

26 03 07, 16:10

24 09 06, 09:59

43

> **From:** Jane McMorrow > **Date:** 3 Feb 2006 16:32 > **To:** David Harradine > **Subject:** *Venue*
>
Hi David, > I know that you have been communicating with Matt and are planning to visit Brighton on the 14th Feb. > Once you have found a venue and finished developing the idea and put together a draft budget (my team will help you with this) we will be in a position to put in an outline application to NESTA. They are waiting to hear from us. > I know that Matt has done lots of work in researching venues for you and I'm sure the 14th will be a really fruitful day. > Over to you at this stage I think. > Best, Jane X

> **From:** David Harradine > **Date:** 14 August 2007 11:10 > **To:** Jane McMorrow > **Subject:** *Venue*
>
hi jane > good to chat on friday. i'm keen to have a look at any alternative venues as soon as possible, so that we can all be clear about where the project will be, and so i can start designing it! if there's any possibility of setting up those visits next week, that'd be great. if it's worth looking at possible venues for

Brilliant at the same time, that'd be great too. also, i will be coming down with ali (our production manager) again, so if it's worth her meeting with your technical/production manager, then that'd be a third great thing... > david x

> **From:** Tanya Ashdown > **Date:** 16 August 2007 12:37 > **To:** David Harradine > **Subject:** *Spaces*
>
Hi David, > I am looking into the possibility of 2 other spaces for you but it is unlikely we will get to visit them by next week. One is the old Fruit and Veg Market (although there is already a queue of people wanting to use that) and the other is Unit 9 of the Terraces on Marine Drive (I'm still trying to find out who actually owns this!). > I'll contact you as soon as I have more info and some possible dates. > Tanya

09 05 06, 14:12

This is a project about walking and waiting. Walking
through town, light's flâneur, waiting for the sun to
set. Walking past sea-views framed by street-ends,
sea's slide show. Waiting for the weather to turn,
waiting for inspiration. Walking in hope of finding it.

09 05 06, 14:21

09 05 06, 14:24

A space that enables the exploration of the dynamic relationship between seeing and moving

A space that makes Movement

> **From:** Tanya Ashdown > **Date:** 29 August 2007 17:41 > **To:** David Harradine > **Subject:** *Spaces*
>
Hi, > Phil and I are going to look at the Terraces Unit tomorrow and we are still waiting to here from the property managers what their schedules are and whether this space will be available to us or not. > The site visit to the Fruit and Veg market is unlikely to happen before 7 Sept now as various people that need to be involved are on leave. > I'll let you know what the unit is like and keep you up to date with availability and access to the fruit and veg market. > Tanya

> **From:** Matt Jones > **Date:** 23 September 2007 15:02 > **To:** David Harradine > Cc: Sophie Pridell > **Subject:** *Spaces*
>
Hi Sophie, David, > It's Matt from the Festival here. I'm afraid my video phone footage of the Terraces space screwed up; it's kind of like The Basement, but much bigger. > Pros: Size, location (next to seafront), atmosphere > Cons: Will not know for a week or two if we can definitely use it, no infrastructure

(except power and water) so will be more expensive to set up (temp toilets, fire safety system etc.) > Tanya and I will see what progress we can make with the management company this week. So, great space, but don't get your hopes up yet! We are still keeping on with the Basement as a fall back. > We'll talk during the week. > Best, Matt

> **From:** Matt Jones > **Date:** 9 October 2007 18:10 > **To:** David Harradine > Cc: Sophie Pridell > **Subject:** *Update*
>
Hi guys, > I wanted to let you know that we are likely to have a decision on the Terraces this Thursday. Our contact is putting it to the three directors of the company then, and he'll come back to us shortly after. > So, at the very least we will have resolution on this by the end of the week - fingers crossed! > Matt

> **From:** David Harradine > **Date:** 9 October 2007 21:07 > **To:** Matt Jones > **Subject:** *re: Update*
>
eeeeeeek! i'm putting on a brave face but i'll be gutted if it doesn't come through. so yes, fingers crossed.

> **From:** Matt Jones > **Date:** 11 October 2007 11:49 > **To:** David Harradine > **Subject:** *Terraces*
>
Sorry to tell you but I thought I'd be blunt - it doesn't look good regarding the Terraces. > Here is the email Tanya received this morning: > *From: Richard Franklin > Sent: 10 October 2007 17:15 > To: Tanya Ashdown > Subject: RE: Brighton Festival - The Terraces - further info > Tanya, > As discussed I have met with the directors of Brighton Seafront Regeneration Ltd and they have unfortunately confirmed that they are aiming to be undertaking extensive construction works throughout the buildings at that time and therefore they cannot commit at this stage. Reluctantly I am therefore afraid that we will have to say no to your request at this time. > Kind Regards, > Richard.*
>
Now, we'll have one last shot at this on Monday when we can next speak with him, but at this stage we'd have to be pretty sceptical of changing their minds. > Let's talk Monday then and make a final decision on the back of our last ditch effort then. > Sorry to be the bearer of sad tidings! > Matt

> **From:** Matt Jones > **Date:** 29 October 2007 16:26 > **To:** David Harradine > Cc: Sophie Pridell > **Subject:** *The Basement*
>
Hi guys, > Although we already knew it, I think it's officially time to put the final nail in the coffin of the larger terraces space and accept that The Basement remains the best bet for An Infinite Line. > It would be good if you could confirm you're happy with this (unless you've developed any other ideas over the last couple of weeks!) so we can begin locking things in with The Basement. > Matt

28 03 07, 11:26

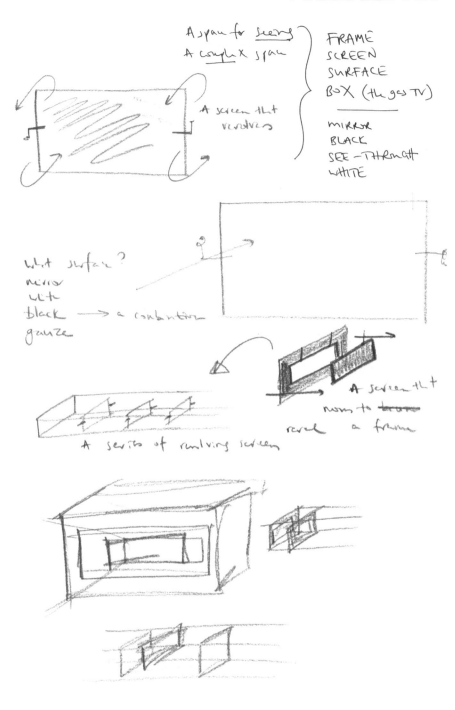

A space for seeing
A complex space

A screen that revolves

FRAME
SCREEN
SURFACE
BOX (the gas TV)

MIRROR
BLACK
SEE-THROUGH
WHITE

What surface?
mirror
white
black ——> a combination
gauze

A series of revolving screens

A screen that moves to reveal a frame

> From: David Harradine > Date: 29 October 2007 17:44 > To: Matt Jones > Subject: re: The Basement
>
hi matt > thanks for confirming this. of course i'm disappointed, but i know that we saw the space in the expectation that it wouldn't work out. at least it's good to be clear, so we can get on with the design process. > for example, we may want the audience to use the existing entrance, i.e not the new foyer entrance, as playing that way round gives us more capacity potential; there's also a large hooved question about a horse, and there are lots of big practical implications that we need to talk through before i can make an informed artistic decision. > the performance/ installation balance is also dependent on various things to do with the venue, with access, and with other uses (or not) of the space during the festival. we also need to talk about capacity for the performances, as of course that will be much more limited in The Basement. > these are all things that we can talk through and sort out. > thanks a lot > david

Here is a moving set, framing these stage pictures (like the streets that frame the view of the sea). How can the set move? How can we configure it? How does it liberate us, limit us, where does it take us? It moves. How does it move me?

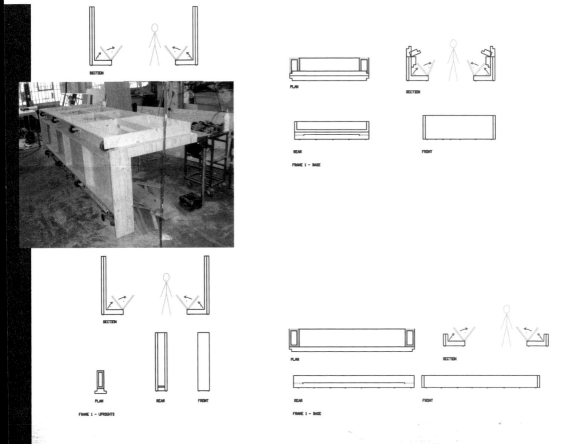

SECTION

PLAN

SECTION

REAR

FRONT

FRAME 1 - BASE

SECTION

PLAN

FRONT

FRAME 1 -

SECTION

PLAN

REAR

FRONT

FRAME 1 - UPRIGHTS

PLAN

SECTION

REAR

FRONT

FRAME 1 - BASE

An Infinite Line: Brighton was a project about light, the particular quality of light in Brighton. Being about light, it was about how we see, how light reveals and transforms a place, and about how the particularities of a place transform how we see, feel, and perceive the light. It was a project about the visual, and about how the visual is linked to the physical, the sensual, the emotional, the visceral, the intellectual, the philosophical and the temporal. The experience of *looking*, of taking time to be attentive in order to *see* a place for what it actually is, and the process of opening oneself up to the possibility of surprise, revelation and *understanding*: these things were at the very heart of the project.

Because of all this, from the outset my ideas for the project were grounded in an assumption that the visual and the processes of making images for the audience to see would be central. Although the piece was much more, in the end, than a 'visual poem' (being, as it was, full of sound, of words; being a physical experience and an intellectual one as well as a visual one) the processes of making images, manipulating light, inventing a set, creating movement and framing my experience of the light as a visually-led 'performance landscape' were the things that most preoccupied me.

This is all part of an ongoing process, not one that was unique to this project. I can't separate any part of my practice from a process of image making. Although much of my work is as a director, I also design (in this case with Ali and Jo), I think all the time about lighting, and I imagine performances as a series of images presented in time. Although the work contains much in addition to images, these things come later.

This process of thinking about images is also, and at the same time, the process of thinking about an idea. It is through images that ideas are revealed. Throughout the writing of project proposals it is images that guide me, that help me see what's possible in a project or in a place. The process of imagining, is also and always a process of imaging. The image and the imagining and the idea and the understanding are one.

    * * *

I am also fascinated by stuff. Objects are always sources of possibility.
I run improvisations like a series of experiments. What are the properties
of these things? What do they know? What can they reveal to us, tell us,
show us? What can we do with them? What can we see? And what can
doing and seeing help us create?

Here is a block of chalk. What can we do with this? How does it move?
How does it make you move? Does it have a sound? How can we make it
have a sound? How does it behave, what are its material properties?
Put these properties in your body. What happens? How does it take light?
How does it feel? How does it make you feel? Show me how it makes you feel.
    Here is a glass sphere. Fill it with water, fill it with haze, fill it with air.
Use your breath to fill it with condensation. How does it dance with you?
Wear it on your head. Speak. Sing. How do these images make me feel?
    Here is a moving set, framing these stage pictures (like the streets that
frame the view of the sea). How can the set move? How can we configure it?
How does it liberate us, limit us, where does it take us? It moves. How does
it move me?
    Here are wineglasses. Can you play them like an instrument? What
happens if you project this film through a glass? How does the glass
refract light? Can you walk on it? Line up these glasses, and walk on them.
(But this image is also a recycled image. We have used it in four previous
projects. Devising is an ongoing process in an ongoing body of work,
and I'm interested in how discoveries from one project can resurface in
another, how images can be used again and again, so that there is a
dialogue through time, between individual projects that are therefore
never entirely lost).

I am fascinated by stuff, and I am fascinated by places, spaces, sites.
Did I want to make the piece for The Basement? Actually, no. I thought it
was too small a space for a project about the light. But we had, in the end,
no alternative. So here we are. A long, low, narrow brick and concrete space.
How do you work with that? How can we make it move? How will it hold
our images? We love that it is a basement, though, that there isn't any light.

* * *

Memory is a screen for re-viewing images from the past.

I remember looking at LED lighting equipment with Ali and Jo. I remember washes of colour over a white screen, over a pile of white chalk, over a body, over a white horse. I remember the sensuality of colour. I remember Mark de-focusing a projector, to replace the image with a block of moving coloured light, a landscape turned to light, film turned abstract. I remember blue, and orange, and grey. I remember Laura trying to move with the rhythm of blue, and orange, and grey. I remember her attempts to become colour, to become light.

* * *

Devising and improvisation are always about creating images *and* about the sensuality of images: the images are made 'right' when they generate sensuality and emotion in the space, in the performers, in me (and in the audience, I hope). I watch David improvise on the bass. It is the image of his playing, his effort, that moves me as much as the sound. I watch these slowly changing coloured lights, barely visible through a narrow slit in a faraway frame in the set, and the slowness moves me, the slowness of the colours changing moves me. I remember how I felt when I was alone with the experience of the light, solitary witness, revelation, and how seeing the sunset's secrets awed me, silenced me, moved me.

Throughout the creation of this project, I wanted to make images that embodied my *feelings* about the light, and images that captured something of the experience of being *in* the light, in Brighton, in the landscape, in the spaces between sea and city and sky. Laura dances the September sunset's colours. We fall silent, awed. We applaud. Here is a body briefly turned to colour and light. Exhausted by that effort, consumed. Here in the rehearsal room, here in the performance, here is an image of the light.

* * *

Throughout the creation of the project, I wanted to make images that on the one hand revealed something about Brighton, about why the light there is like it is, about the particularity of place and landscape that renders the light unique; and on the other that created poetry, created the inexplicable, the inarticulable, the strange: images that created something unique to the performance. I wanted the project to be both a response to the real place Brighton, and an imaginary space, a new space.

I wanted to make a space that was never still. A space that kept changing shape and changing colour. Mercurial, fluid, protean. A space full of objects and light and lights and wind and bodies and breath and music and sound. A complex space, littered, glittering. Shiny and sensual; too bright and grey dull; plastic and chalk. A new image and a memory. A collision of light and design and space, pushing through time.

(pp.56–7)
The Frames, *An Infinite Line:
Brighton*, the performance,
May 2008

June. No photographs: camera stolen. But I remember the blazing ball of the sun flare across the camera's screen, the dark blue infinitely deep dark sky around the furious ball of light, the dirty white teeth of the cliffs.

Saturday 20th January, 3.15pm.
And then, standing from the
bench and stepping forward:
there, at the end of this street,
low down, just a
the road itself, a
street, the sun, a
molten liquid rag
light. Gold, yellov
brilliance in the
powdery mist, o
Walk down the f
street contains t
next: the sun. Th
the next. The su
city, bedding do
of Hanover, up h
hill meets the hil
the city crouche
powdery light. T
green. Light bro
lowering, powde
surface here; he
liquidmetal light

SINGLE SOURCE OF LIGHT

There'll be objects, materials, a kind of installation, which is the set
(it will also be a kind of playground for the performers, and playing in it is
how we'll devise the performance). There'll be a very large, very powerful
wind machine, and haze machines, and smoke, and a system that will
make it rain in the space, playing the role of the weather. There'll be a very
large, very ornate, very beautiful chandelier, playing the role of the sun.

From fourth project proposal for Brighton Festival, July 2006

A dazzlingly bright backlight, blinding like the sun.

A bank of builder's work lights set up at the back of the space, 10 squares of dazzling light coming though the mist from a haze machine.

An industrial floodlight behind a white cloth, slowly brightening, flooding the space with a hard white metallic light.

A theatre light, pointed direct from the back towards the audience.

Light experiments: Ali, Laura, Jamie, David and Joseph, August 2007 R&D

Laura and Sam,
August 2007 R&D

(pp.64–5)
**The Horizon Beginning
Finally to Appear**,
An Infinite Line: Brighton,
the performance, May 2008

Saturday 23rd September, 7.04pm.
On the golf course at Roedean,
high up, looking back at the city.
   The city is white, pink, very pale
blue. The sky: in
description: orar
brown, bronze, re
pale blue, blueg
turquoise, pale c
everything and e
It's beautiful. Th
heavy, high, bec
threatening, unc
setting sun. Gre
rippled crumplec
striated, then so
colours changin
light dimmer eve
to see: visibly fa
notebook, leavir
colours begin to
dark, turning gre
two immense cc
steelybluegrey c
behind the horiz
   The sea is wei
by that sky. The
texture of silk. It
choir, but distan
awed. Also, like
And cold. There'
from the East, a
the Palace Pier,
the striped and c
Western sky.
...

7.12pm. The sky a
again, grey, Sep

COLOUR

What colour is the city? What colour is the sky? What colour is the sea?
What is the texture of the light? What is the sound of the light? How do
I feel? What's the weather like? Where is the light, now?
   How do these colours move? How does 'red' dance? How does
'grey' walk? How does 'skyblue' feel, make me feel, how does it move,
how does it make me move?
   Movement, bodies: trying to inhabit this space. Human bodies,
in the light, in the mist, being colour, becoming colour, becoming light.

From 'Thoughts on the Project', January 2008

23 09 06, 19:02

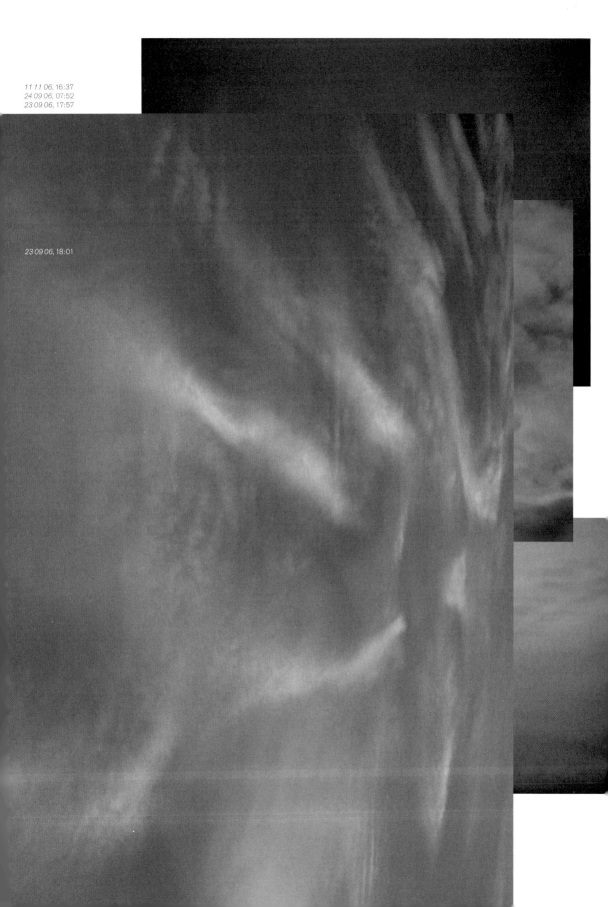

11 11 06, 16:37
24 09 06, 07:52
23 09 06, 17:57

23 09 06, 18:01

using LED light to backwash a screen,
so as to be in control of an
infinite array of colour. Each
movement of the performers,
a different colour. Each new
position: change. Each sweep of
the arm: change. Endless colour.
Endless change.

Monday 26th March, 10.10am.
Crossing the crest of this ridge at
the golf course, the city appears.
At first sight, the white blocks of
the buildings lea
green and blue.
chalky, hit and b   CHALK
light from the Ea
quixotic: now gr
blue, now grey a
horizon still smu
still blurred, pow

...

6.30pm. Running
the clocks sprar
Running East, tc
the marina. A ba
spans the entire
orangepink ball
the Western hor
here, white (yell
browngreywhite
gathered and he
wetted, turned t
paste, cement-li
grey. The horizo
band of lighter v
the Marina to th
parallel to the b
twenty yards ou
sky, a ribbon of I
A cloud, underlit
refracted sun.

...

Monday 8th May,
The racecourse,
Pale brown soil,
Flint, chalky flint
of sheep.

...

Thursday 29th Ju
Saltdean, Cliffs,
of chalk.
   Teeth.
   The hard whit
white (yellow wh
dirty white) rock
   At sea, a millic
ripple, each und
breeze-brought
water tipped wit
shimmering ligh

This environment will consist of objects (such as blocks of chalk and
chalk rubble) that evoke the physical geography particular to Brighton;
it will contain meteorological elements that imitate the external weather
conditions in an interior space (mist, wind, rain, hard bright light); it will
contain elements that suggest the colour and form of the buildings of
the city, and of the sky and sea.

From third project proposal for Brighton Festival, March 2006

27 03 07, 10:26
20 07 06, 12:34

12 10 06, 16:21

> **From:** ali beale >
Date: 4 July 2007
19:39 > **To:** David
Harradine > **Subject:**
chalk
>
Hello, > Just a bit of
an update, spoke to
Mark at the Chalk
quarry, we could get
a chunk of chalk one
metre cubed but this
would weigh 1½ tons
but unfortunately we
wouldn't be able to
get it down the stairs
into the venue, or take
it in the lift – you need
forklifts and pallets
on solid ground to
move that kind of
weight around. >
However if we were to
go for some smaller
pieces 'dustbin size'
(not entirely sure
exactly how big that
is) we would get 4 or
5 of them to a ton and
they come in about
£30 per ton. Obviously
we would also need
transport/delivery on
top of this. > There
seems to be quite a
few options with size
shape etc, Mark has
suggested a visit
before we buy any-
thing which I think
sounds a good idea.
He has also offered to
take photos of various
chunks but I think it
would be better if you
could see them in
person? Do you have
any time free?!! >
Sorry all my emails
can't be as exciting
and positive as the
horsey ones... > Hope
all's lovely at the Lyric,
> speak soon, > ali x

> **From:** ali beale >
Date: 7 July 2007
13:06 > **To:** David
Harradine > **Subject:**
Brighton up-date
>
Hi David, >
Wednesday morning –
Somborne Chalk
Quarry > Mark will
be available on
Wednesday morning
to show us various
blocks of chalk of
different sizes and
weights. Obviously
the weight is quite
crucial as we need
to be able to get the
chalk into the space.
I'll come too on
Wednesday, are you
able to drive? >
Speak soon, Ali

74

a ridge or a mound
of salt of salt

or a ridge
of chalk rubble

The chalk: writing, erasing, starting again, overwriting, palimpsest, writing, erasing, starting again, smudge, blur, erase, start again. The language given physical form.

Chalk experiments:
Jamie B, Jamie M,
Laura, Joseph & David,
August 2007 R&D

Light shining on the blocks – like a micro-version of Brighton (the blocks), the sun/light shining onto the city surface with the (chalk) sea in front. Cine postcards projected onto the chalk; snatches of words, of information, notes recording an experience of the light.

Chalk was one of the key design elements throughout the development of the project. It became clear really early on in the research visits that the geology of the South Downs – the massive amount of chalk in and around Brighton – was one of the key things that made the light in Brighton appear like it does, and we wanted to show this by working with chalk in the performance.

During the R&D, we built mounds of chalk rubble like miniature cliffs; we dropped curtains of chalk dust and projected cine film onto them; we created a beautiful, beautiful image of a projected seagull flying over a hand-held moving block of chalk; we built walls, knocked walls down; threw chalk rocks around; hung the rocks from steel cable, and with contact microphones attached to the cable played the rocks like a musical instrument (I remember the ensemble playing *What a Wonderful World* on a piece of hung chalk: quite a moment).

Much of the material we made during the R&D and the rehearsal period involved chalk. But then we started working with a horse. He found it hard enough to move on a polished floor without the added factor of chalk dust. The castors the set moved on wouldn't roll over chalk rubble. I couldn't find a place in the eventual structure for that image of the seagull (I still regret this: it was such a beautiful image).

And so in the end, we didn't really work with chalk at all, except for a moment, as Laura danced the Roedean sunset, when Jamie built a chalk town around her and then moved it away as her dance became more wild.

In the project as a whole, the chalk appeared in other ways: the book was designed to resemble a block of chalk; in the installation, each film was projected onto chalk, like a moving postcard. But in the performance, hardly anything at all.

To devise is to create, but not everything you create makes it into the final cut. And so the chalk was all but cut.

... IMAGE

How did we create images?

Since the work we make is design-led, the creation of images is a central focus of our daily practice. Images tend to be created in one of two ways:

1 **Through play and improvisation:**

usually by working with an object (such as a mirrored tile); a material (such as chalk); within the restrictions of a given space or architecture; or with light.

2 **Through a director-led process:**

I will often come to a project with an existing set of visual ideas which I want to create in the space. There will be an image that I might have seen in a photograph, which might have emerged during a research process, which suggests itself as a way of articulating an idea, or which will linger from a previous project. Working with performers, light, space, objects and materials as the matter from which an image will be constructed, I will compose and direct, without going through long processes of play and improvisation. When working in this way, it's important that I can explain to people why we're making these images, so that there can be a sense of understanding and a sort of ownership for those people who are involved in the doing of them. Ultimately, it's the performers who need to present the material to an audience, and they have to be able to trust that the material belongs in the piece.

In both these processes, it's really useful to have visual reference material to hand in the room. The walls tend to get covered in photos, drawings, crappy little sketches of moments from improvisations, clippings, copies of paintings: anything that might be a stimulus and a guide in finding ways of building visual material in the space. I also find this accumulated stuff a kind of reassurance – when I'm feeling uninspired and unsure what to do next there's always something there to refer to, to say, "let's look at that" or "let's try to recreate this."

It's hard to analyse the second approach, as it's really to do with instinct, and a very personal process. It's easier to deconstruct the first – the one based in a collaborative play and improvisation.

In the performance there was an image of Laura beneath a 'skirt' of mirrored tiles, suggestive of the sea, or of drowning.

HOW DID WE MAKE THIS IMAGE?

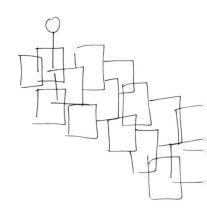

It went something like this:

We had the tiles in the room, as I had wanted a material that evoked the harsh, metallic, highly reflective surface of the sea that I had seen so often during my research visits. We had looked at different materials during early R&D, and the tiles were chosen as they were robust, portable, could be configured in different ways, and weren't too expensive.

Early in devising we spent half a day exploring different ways of working with the tiles. This led to a number of different images. Each of these images emerged through the same process of structured physical play:

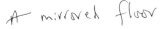

> Explore the material, try things out, see how it moves, how it makes you move, experiment, configure it in different ways, put it in different places.

> I'd suggest ideas, "Can you try this?", and feed back on what I was seeing.

> Push against the problems: don't give up when something doesn't want to work, when the material resists your manipulation or play, or if it causes practical problems. For example, working with piles of chalk dust and rubble, one of the immediate issues was that the chalk got everywhere, becoming very messy, and covered the performers in dirt. Rather than stopping to clean up, we allowed this to become the focus of this play, with improvisations encouraged that made more and more mess. This led us to talking about landscape and chaos.

> Take a lot more time than you want to: persist, take time to see possibilities, go beyond the point when you think there is nothing more to discover (but be aware of how tiring it is for the people who are doing the physical work, who can't see the things that you're seeing, nor know what you're looking for).

> Keep observing, respond, make suggestions, direct, give stimulus when things start to flag.

> Solve technical problems (e.g. how to hold or manipulate something).

> Try again, keep going, persist.

> Trust your instinct: if the thing which you want to take forward leaps out at you, know that you have recognised it.

Throughout these initial stages, I would take photographs of the improvisations, or make quick (and very rubbish) sketches in my notebook. Synne filmed everything we did, so we could always go back and remind ourselves how we had done something. It's impossible to remember everything you discover when running these long improvisations.

With the tiles, this process was repeated several times, in different ways:

a period of play with them laid out like a catwalk;

using them as a mirror to bounce back a light which lit someone moving on them;

using them as a dance floor, a space that limited and suggested physical improvisations;

the tiles reflected

laying them against and across the other elements of the set, to start to build three-dimensional structures;

Jamie Bradley and David trying to build a box, a cube, around Laura, a space of confinement;

laying the tiles on the floor, gradually building up like scales around Laura, then seeing how they move.

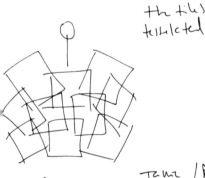

surface

Jamie / David
Lifting them into
a shifting 3D
structure / surface

Each of these improvisations was interesting in its own way, but the final one was the one that struck me most, as it most directly evoked something that I remembered from being outside in the city: *looking at the rippling shifting surface of the metallic sea*. It was also technically difficult to do: for Jamie and David, controlling and manipulating the tiles was awkward, and this made a lot of sense in relation to the idea of 'struggling to find a way to respond to the light' that had become a central motif in the piece. So this was the image we developed. Once we had chosen this idea, we developed it through a process like this:

> **Respond with sound.**

All our improvisations tended to include sound and light, but often in a very open and fluid, changeable way. Once we had selected this image, I spent more time with Mark and Jamie McCarthy exploring sound possibilities that linked to the image: the sound of that harsh, cold, beautiful, metallic sea. We had to focus on the violin (Jamie) and the electronic processing (Mark) as David was working physically in the image, so unable to play: that simple limitation bringing its own possibilities.

Video documentation
of improvisations
(left)

> **Find the rhythm, quality, potential meanings.**

What does this image mean? How does it feel? How can it articulate something about the experience of the light? How should it be paced, how quick, how languid? How should Laura move? How does the sound help us find this quality? Is sound strengthening the image, or working against it? Is this the right sound, or do we need to discover something different? Where in the space do we locate the image? (we place it far upstage and it takes on a quality of a dream, of a memory of a real experience, of something from the past).

> **Add light.**

Although we worked with light all the time (I find it impossible to get a sense of material without being able to see how it works and feels technically) we would focus in on lighting once an image became concrete. Jo (the lighting designer) would be trying different ideas as we were playing, some of which fitted well with the physical/musical work, some of which didn't. Once we'd got a clearer sense of the structure, rhythm, musicality of an image, we'd start to develop the lighting design within it. In design-led work like this, the lighting has a massive impact on how things feel and look, so we always had to be careful that the light didn't take the material in a different direction, or to know why we wanted the light to change something if we let it.

Day 2 of devising: Jamie B, Jamie M, Laura and David

> **Structure, compose.**

Once we felt we had found the essence of the image, we focused on technicalities and the shape of it – the journey through the image from emergence to disappearance.

How does it appear?

How do we build it?

Who does what, and how, and when?

How does it end, how do we dismantle it?

How long does it last?

Of course, this composition changed through the process: building a fairly complete image in devising is one thing, but the image had to adapt in order for it to fit in with other elements of the final version of the piece.

> **Add detail, refine, direct.**

Once we'd found an outline structure, we would zoom in on the detail, to physical precision, timing, performance qualities: "Can you bring on *this* object from *that* direction and place it *here* at this point, at the same time as *he* is doing *that*..."

One of the problems of image-based work like this is that the performers usually have no idea how it looks, and can find it hard to sense the difference between those rhythms or qualities or actions that work in the context of the image, and those that don't. Having a directorial eye is vital, and having the video recording – so that the performers could step out and see what they were doing – was really useful.

The video functioned as a memory, it allowed us to review something to see how it worked, to solve technical problems if we couldn't get it to work a second time, and it brought confidence to the performers, allowing them to see the material from the audience's point of view, and to believe me when I told them, "It looks good." The video became a mechanism for development, for sharing, and for empowerment.

Inevitably in a piece about light, some of the images we made focused very much on light itself, rather than on another object or material. When we wanted to work with light as a material, a kind of insubstantial 'stuff', we still worked through all the same stages outlined above, only we started with light – with a beam of light, with coloured light, with a particular kind of light source, with cine projections used as moving light, with an object emitting light, or with darkness.[1]

Every time we came to make an image, we started with a stimulus, played, spotted the thing we liked, and developed it. That doesn't mean that every image we created was in the performance: some of the strongest visuals didn't make the final edit.[2]

[1] There's more about this in the section **On Light**.

[2] **On Structure** has more about how we selected material and composed it, how we made decisions and how we gradually built the piece.

... LIGHT

How did we work with light and lighting?

An *Infinite Line: Brighton* was about light, so on some level, everything that appeared in the performance was linked to light, even the sound, even the way the set moved, even the horse. We generated a huge amount of physical material in direct response to light. The text (the notes from my research visits) described light, and was used as a stimulus for music, for image, for action. Even in the dark underground space of The Basement, even when we were working in darkness, the idea of working with light permeated everything.

Very early on, we understood that the performance was not going to be a recreation of the natural light out there in the city. Although there were moments in it which suggested a glimpse of the real light in Brighton, generally we were more concerned to make a piece that on the one hand recreated the *experience* of being in a city whose light is characterised by relentless change, and on the other hand foregrounded the challenge of making an art event in response to the light in the first place.

WHY MAKE A PIECE ABOUT THE LIGHT WHEN THE LIGHT ITSELF IS ALREADY SO BEAUTIFUL AND SO EXTRA-ORDINARY?

In thinking about light in these ways, we focused again and again on the idea of translation, on how one thing can become another, how light can manifest itself through other things. In much of the work I'd been doing prior to making this project, I had also been working really closely with Jo to explore ways of placing light at the very start, or the very centre, of creative processes. We had made site-specific light installations, and performance events which took light as their focus and their starting point, and in a lot of these projects we had worked with light as a material substance which can be brought into a rehearsal space and played with, or improvised around, in just the same way as one can play or improvise with a physical object, or with another performer. This principle – of the centrality of light in devising – was one that we brought to *An Infinite Line: Brighton*. These are some of the things we did:

Light and Movement

We talked a lot, throughout the R&D and later devising, about the idea of 'becoming light': ways in which qualities of light could be embodied by the performers, either through their actions, or the sounds they made, or through their actual physical presence and movement. We did a lot of physical work on responding to materials, generally guided by a set of questions:

what is the rhythm of this material?

does it move fast or slow?

what is its direction, is it an upwards material, or downwards; horizontal or vertical?

what shape is it, is it sharp, or flat, or jagged, or smooth?

The materials we talked about were often meteorological:

fog, rain, wind, water, mist.

This process was not one of learning rules or of trying to find the correct answer to these sorts of questions, but much more about finding a kind of liberation that allowed the performers, especially Laura and Jamie Bradley, to respond instinctively, to just try

something. We spent a couple of days during the R&D working with dancers – Robin and Delphine – and their physical freedom and technical experience was really vital in helping Jamie and Laura discover a kind of free and impulsive physical response. As we moved through various experiments working with light, we continued to respond in this way. We had these LED lights that could produce an almost infinite array of different colours, and would run long improvisations where they would slowly change, with the performers responding physically to each colour. The material this led to was extremely abstract, usually a sort of strange dance, and absolutely worked with this guiding principle of 'becoming light'. Responding to and directing this material, I would never be thinking about what was right or wrong, but only looking for things that were strong in and of themselves: if someone discovered a movement in response to a flickering green light that was an interesting movement, it didn't matter at all whether or not it 'was green'. The light was a stimulus for the creation of other things.

Light and Sound

One of these other things was sound and music. In the same way that I asked Jamie Bradley and Laura to respond physically to different sorts of light, I would endlessly ask Jamie McCarthy and David and Mark to respond through sound:

what is the sound of blue?

what frequency is red, what instrument, what kind of sound?

as we watch this light at the back of the space brighten and become blinding, what do we hear?

can you make a slowly developing sonic landscape that has the structure of the rising and the setting of the sun?

Light and Projection: Moving Light

Mark and I had spent a lot of time between the 2007 R&D and the devising period returning to Brighton and making short cine films of the city, the sea, the sky and the light. I called it our light harvest, and we were gathering these images to use in the cine film installation that would be one of the three manifestations of *An Infinite Line: Brighton*. We had also decided, after some experiments in the R&D, to use some of these films in the performance.

There is something about the materiality of cine film which feels totally different to video projection. It's a more poetic, more tangible medium, which has a different sort of presence (like the difference between a digital photograph and a film photograph); there is something about the physical, chemical presence of light in the film.

In the performance, we knew we wanted to use the films as a way for moving images to interrupt other material: sudden glimpses of clouds, the sea, a seagull, the sun flaring up in the darkness of the basement.[1]

We also wanted to use them purely as a light source, as a way of illuminating other elements of the performance. In this respect, working with cine projectors was also useful, as they were portable, easily manipulated, and could easily be controlled and moved by the performers during the piece. We did a lot of playing with the projectors – defocusing them, projecting through wineglasses, onto water, onto haze, onto each other, onto Phoenix the horse; bouncing their moving coloured light off the mirrored tiles, onto the set, onto chalk.

Light Objects

We mainly focused on light itself, as an immaterial substance. At various points we also explored the physical presence of sources of light, and this especially developed in images of the ensemble lighting each other, handling lights, moving projectors, dealing with the mechanics of making the image.

We also worked with light-emitting objects:

light wire (simply a plastic wire with an element through the centre that emits light when an electric charge runs through it);

phosphorescent power, which we covered Jamie Bradley with before shining a light on him (he didn't glow in the dark as I'd expected, and it was a ridiculous ritual, one that we never repeated).

This was a different sort of physical play, and one that opened up performance lighting to non-theatrical sources.

[1] I've described in *On Image* how we would go through processes of play to create visual material, and we worked with the projectors in the way that I've detailed there.

Technicalities: The Stuff of Light

Working in this way with light brings its own demands. We needed to be working in a space where lighting equipment was present from day one, and we had to make sure that there was someone in the team whose job it was to control and manipulate the light in rehearsals and devising. This person tended to be either Jo or Ali (the production manager), although at times it would be me, occasionally it would be the performers, and, because we were working with the cine films as a source of light, it was frequently Mark.

In terms of staffing, technical resources, time and budget, the decision to work like this proved costly. We were working with a laptop-based control system that was meant to be flexible and responsive, and particularly useful in relation to controlling the colour changing of the LED lights, but no one was totally proficient in using it, so it really slowed us down. This technically resourced approach brings huge benefits in terms of being able to create and develop quite complete material very quickly, but we had to have the patience of saints during those frequent periods when we were wrestling with the technology of control. You need to allow a lot of time for technical problem solving when working in this way: we would frequently spend half an hour setting things up for a two minute improvisation. Was it worth it? Often it was, but not always. It was very difficult for the performers, who would frequently lose energy and momentum. The physical and emotional conditions of the space in which one works has a huge impact on the process, on the material, and on the wellbeing of the company. In this project, those conditions

were partly determined by this technically led way of working, and also by the fact of being in a dark basement. We developed strategies for dealing with this – I would always try to remember to send people up to see daylight during a break, and to release them during these periods of technical preparation.

Light and The Light

Although these ways of translating light to other phenomena (movement, sound, music, film) were the focus for most of the devising process, there were also qualities in the natural light in Brighton that it felt vital to bring directly into the piece in some way. Even though we never wanted to be figurative or representational with the light or the design ("Here is an image of someone sitting on the beach"), I did want to include some key things that very directly evoked the light outside:

> the metallic surface of the sea;
>
> the bright dazzling light of a low winter sun that lifts up behind the city;
>
> the sodium orange glare of a streetlight. [2]

These uses of light became anchor points in the performance, moments of recognition for the audience that punctuated the abstract, oblique, non-literal material that formed most of the piece.

[2] There's more about these images in the chapter Light, Design, Space.

One of the most thrilling and challenging aspects of *An Infinite Line:
Brighton* was the presence of a horse in the performance. Phoenix:
a spotted white stallion. This chapter explores some of the ideas, problems
and possibilities that underscored Phoenix's presence, and describes
the process which led to the decision to work specifically with a horse.
The text section is structured in multiple voices, describing *The Narrative*,
The Discovery of Why, and *The Experience*. *The Narrative* describes the
journey which led to Phoenix's role in the project. *The Discovery of Why*
unravels some of the conceptual realisations that helped us make sense
of this role. *The Experience* recalls the lived encounter: how it felt for us
to be working with a horse, how it felt to be in the presence of an animal.

08 05 06, 15:42

In the Presence of Animals   [92–113]

A bird in flight.
This is an image of return, ot
of movement and change.

animal, alien,
nature; pure presence,
inexplicable, independent
of all process, of all art.

> **From:** Ali Beale >
Date: 7 July 2007
13:06 > **To:** David
Harradine > **Subject:**
Brighton up-date
>
Hi David, > I've
booked you some
appointments for next
week: Monday 11am,
Impact Falconry. >
I have arranged for
you to meet James
Long at their yards
to have a look at the
birds they have. He
is their film/theatre/
events person. > The
idea is that you go
and have a look at
the birds to see if you
think they would be
any good, he said you
can then get some
lunch and have a chat
with him about the
project. This is a free
consultation and
then if you are still
interested we can get
a quote for the R&D
and the show.
>
>
>
>
>
>
>
>
>
>
>
>
>
>
>
>
>
>

Natural ;
Always do

THE thor
↳ th

**Th
cor**

Ribena's Har
Find out mo

get
sheep
Horse

and always the same

gr is a struggle to expres

FLOW : an
exchange btween
netme system

A HORSE

> **From:** Sophie Pridell > **Date:** 13 July 2007 15:56 > **To:** David Harradine > **Subject:** *Baaaa*
>
I just had a long chat with Jenny at Court Gardens Farm in Ditchling and she is really happy to help in any way she can but doesn't think bringing 'untrained' sheep to the space is going to work. She thinks they will just be terrified and huddle looking sad in the corner. She suggested that you come to the farm and she will bring in some older ewes for you to have a close look at (you could come en masse or bring a couple of the team if you think it would be useful). She can also chat about the different options e.g. getting hold of sheep that were bottle fed as lambs so less twitchy (their orphans go to another farmer she can contact) this certainly sounds like a good idea for next year if you decide to have some woolly friends in the piece. > The best days would be Thursday 2 or Wed 8 for this visit (I would love it to be Wed 8 as I could come down too but you may want to go for the first week). Let me know and I will get back to her. > Soph x

>
>
>
> The horse is booked for the 7th, it is actually £500 not £450. Apparently the steps won't be a problem, and as requested I've asked for the biggest whitest one! > Speak soon, All

95

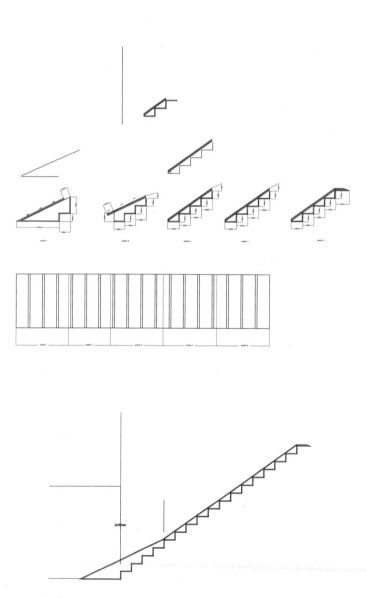

> **From:** Kevin Smith >
Date: 17 July 2007
10:29 > **To:** Ali Beale >
Subject: *RE: Horse Hire
for Brighton*
>

Hi Ali > Thanks for the
width of steps. Horse
will have no problem
with the width. We've
been trying to think of
a safe way for the horse
to get down because of
the amount of steps and
size of them, we want to
make it as easy and safe
as poss. We've come up
with the idea of putting
rubber matting on each
step to stop any slipping,
is this possible for you
to arrange? The horse is
shod at the moment but
we can take the shoes
off if required. > Once
the horse has gone
through the perform-
ance rehearsal once or
twice, it will be used to
the lights dark etc and
should be fine. Rain it's
definitely used to, it
lives in north Wales
(always raining). Also
smoke once it's done it
a few times > It can be
untethered but we do
need to know what the
horse is needed to do. >
The actors can interact
with the horse, ie touch,
stroke and even move
it but this can't be done
if you want a horse to
look dangerous and
wild as the two things
are totally different for
on stage. We can make
it look unkempt instead
of the usual groomed
appearance if that
helps. > Kevin

We built a ramp to make it possible for a ton of horse to walk safely down a steep wooden staircase.

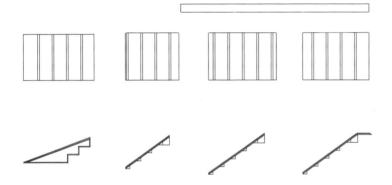

Ramp Notes

- The ramp needs to fit onto stairs with no movement

- The horse weighs approx one ton, with the weight all on the surface area of a hoof. There must be no give in the ramp beneath the horses hoof.

- Top of the ramp from 2 sheets laminated 18mm ply.

- The underside of the ply should have a layer of underlay to dampen the sound.

- The top of the ramp covered with a layer of black ribbed rubber with 2' x 2' strips on top.

- The bottom section slides in separately, it needs four complete formers.

- The three sections above hinge onto the side strip, these sections and the side strip all have the same profile.

- Three medium duty toggle clamps hold sections together at the opposite edge to the hinge.

The Narrative

....

It starts with a dog.

It starts with walking, roaming the hills behind Roedean school, searching out a vantage point, a point of view, a place from which to see the light.

It starts with a dog.

The hills behind Roedean; the bench at the end of Charlotte Street (why this bench? Because it's close to my B&B. Why this B&B? Because I could stay there with a dog); on the beach to the East of the Palace Pier; on the end of the pier; in Hanover, high up where the hill meets the hill; on St James's Street; in the Pavilion Gardens; the white terraces of Clifton. Like poles, these places magnetise me back again and again, repetitive and regular.

And so today, I am re-walking the path from Roedean up to the golf course. Me, my notebook, my camera, and my dog, with whom this part of the story starts. It starts with a dog.

As I walk my slow walk, half looking up at the sky, half looking down at the chalky path, trying to keep a footing while me and the camera, three eyes and a mouth open to the sky, take in the light, she stiffens and runs, alert, scenting sheep, searching out rabbits, tense, all eyes, all perception and presence. We turn off the path, into an empty field, climb the hill to gain a higher vantage point, to look back over the fields to see the colour of the sea. At the top, I gaze my slow, trying-to-see-and-trying-to-understand gaze. She stands looking in the other direction. She's a whippet, a sight hound: her gaze has steel focus,

| **The Discovery** of **Why**　　　The Experience

....

sharp, killer instinct still rising to the surface despite domestication and breeding. **She is purely present in the landscape, part of the grass, made of chalk, earthy.** Being here, she seems to be entirely separate from me, this animal that shares my house, sleeps on my bed. She seems to be a part of this place, connected to the nature that still vibrates beneath her London-living skin.

There's nothing wild about this animal. My pet. But in this moment, with the memory of aggressive gulls around the pier, and the steel stare of a dog on a scent, **I feel the wild indifference of nature.**

I feel the wild indifference of the light.

I come to Brighton with my notebooks and my camera and my questions, my process, my art. I come here to try to understand the light, to work out what I want to say. I roam the city, return to these places, walk, sit, write, look, look, look, wait, watch, try to see. I come to try to understand, so that I can make something, so that I can make something that makes a difference to how other people see. **And the light remains indifferent.**

The light in Brighton, it strikes me early on, is beautiful. Extraordinary. A harsh metallic reflectivity capped with a grey-blue liquid sky. How can I make anything that approaches this? Why make a piece about the light when the light is already so extraordinary, and already so totally indifferent? The city, indifferent. These places, not waiting for me, indifferent.

And an animal, other, elsewhere, infinitely strange and separate

from me. And, despite her shows of affection (which I know are only survival instinct rolled up in pack behaviour), utterly indifferent.

At which point I wonder if there should be an animal in the performance.

At which point I wonder if an animal might somehow remind us that we can never make anything as extraordinary as the light.

At which point I wonder if an animal could stand in for landscape, for weather, for light.

At which point I wonder if an animal would embody indifference.

And so I did this, and I remember:

Visiting a falconry. A bird of prey? Another killer stare, all eyes, watching. Like my human attentiveness to this place, my attempts to really see the place and light, only amplified, magnified a thousand times. I imagine a white falcon. A white owl. A white eagle. In the falconry, caged birds (so it starts to feel wrong), looking out with murder in their eyes. Mindless, pure vision, pure perception. Later, it feels completely wrong. Too dangerous. Too small. Too expensive. Too caged.

But there's something about whiteness. White, like the chalk on this path, like the chalk cliffs here to the East of the Marina. White like the scudding clouds and turning waves. White like the architecture of the city.

I remember visiting a sheep farm. The sheep belong to some of Sophie's friends. I go with Mark, to film the sheep, gathering material to play with in the development workshops. Might there be a flock of sheep in the space? Indifferent? No: they live by a philosophy of ignorant fear. A nervous energy that would be impossible to work with. And there's something ridiculous about a sheep. Although they do have the colour scheme of the landscape, brown and flint and filthy white.

The South Downs. Grazing sheep and white horses cut into the landscape.

And so, we come to the idea of a horse. Something powerful, dangerous, frightening (I have always been afraid of horses). A white horse carved into the chalk of the South Downs. The turning waves of the sea. The sea, 'la mer', a horse.

We decide to invite a horse to join us for a day during the August 2007 R&D. Jo has been working on a film (when he's not lighting performances with me he's a designer for film and television) that used horses, and he recommends a couple of wranglers (Kevin and Cindy) who live in Wales and provide animals to the entertainment industry. Ali gets in touch. Is it possible? How do we do it? Can we get a horse into a basement? Do you have a horse that's white? Can you bring your biggest whitest horse? Do you have a horse with a temperament that will tolerate a strange, chaotic performance piece; a horse that can join us for a day of explorations? Which horse? What will it cost? How will you get to Brighton from Wales? When can you come?

Between the idea and the exploration, these things happen:

We exchange emails about timing, and cost, and access.

Ali sends plans of the staircase that we'll be taking the horse down when he arrives.

Kevin and Cindy build a replica of the staircase in concrete on their farm, so that the horse can practise walking down the steps into an imaginary basement.

I exchange emails about ideas. Will the horse be able to see in the dark? Will we be able to work with loud music? With haze? With bright lights? Can I see what it looks like if I project an image of the sea onto his flank? Is he dangerous? Who will look after him? Who will control him?

We talk about horseshoes, discuss the structure of the basement floor.

No one in the company knows about the horse. Only me, Ali, Jo, Sophie, Louise and Sam. I want to see what happens when people encounter a horse in the basement with no idea he's going to be there.

August: the day he'll be arriving. I tell the company to gather on the beach at 9.45, say that I will call them and ask them to come to the venue when we're ready. I tell them we're preparing the space.

8.30 am. Kevin and Cindy and Phoenix and another horse that's Phoenix's travelling companion arrive. We keep people away from the door of the venue, so that he's not disturbed as he walks down the stairs. Cindy practises walking down the stairs (she'll be leading him down). Phoenix gets out of the truck. He goes through the door. He puts a hoof on the top step. The step, being made of wood not concrete, slightly flexes. He refuses to walk down.

Four hours go by. He refuses to walk down.

Ali goes to the wood merchant around the corner. Buys wood to build a ramp. She builds a ramp. Two hours later, Cindy leads Phoenix down the ramp.

I call the company. I tell them to come to the venue and wait outside. We plan to lead them down in darkness, and use light to reveal Phoenix. I imagine our future audience: the shock of being confronted with a horse.

They enter. Darkness. **A flash of light. A horse. The shock of being confronted with a horse.** Impossible. Extraordinary. I ask each person to walk the length of the space. To meet Phoenix. I ask Laura first. I don't know she's terrified of horses. It being Laura, she goes anyway. **They can't even begin to approach him. Icarus. Burned by the sun.**

We improvise (how do you become horse? How does he move? Move like him. Play for him. How can we light him? Can he be part of the ensemble? Speak to him. Touch him. Don't touch him).

We are exhausted. Exhilarated. Happy. We have to do this.

I can picture him in everything. He could just be. Being here. Present. **A reminder of something other. Part of this but separate; inside, but out: elsewhere.** This moment. The end of the day. People resting, moving, tidying up, clearing his shit. **He stands. Absolutely still, absolutely just himself, just over there. Like the sea. Massive. Always present.**

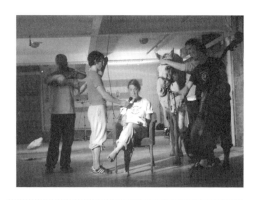

| SYNNE: is this real?

LAURA: The lights snapped on momentarily (a green fluorescent) and I got a flash of a horse burned on my retina in the following black-out. And then cried.

His phenomenal stillness. When we first improvised around him, we couldn't get anywhere near his weight and stillness. He seemed to cut through the air of the space with his stillness and made it thick and heavy.

Phoenix is a thing of wonder, and his presence in the dark basement is unreal. His slow emergence out of the dark makes the sight of him decidedly more uncanny; we recognise him as a horse yet he seems unfamiliar and strange at the same time. There is something both revealing and profound about the way in which his presence touches us,

Considerations:

Do we need an animal, a horse, Phoenix? Can we evoke the indifference and strange presence of nature in another way?

We have this image of a flying gull that Mark filmed, grainy and slow, filmed on cine film, projected by a hand held cine-projector. The image has a materiality, a presence. It's sad, beautiful, slow, melancholic. It is nature. It is change. It is time. It is light. Do we need a live animal when we have this?

But why risk trying another way that might not work when we know Phoenix is a way that works?

How will he be revealed to the audience?

If we want him to simply be present in the space in his indifferent animal skin, how do we also manage his presence as another body, occupier of space, in a space that is constantly moving? How do we move him around, or around him? What does a horse mean?

Practical solutions we need to find:

Where will he be in this tiny venue when he's not on stage?

Where will he be stabled? Where will Kevin and Cindy stay? Where will they park the truck during the performance?

He's not housetrained. What will be the procedure if he goes to the toilet during the performance?

Problems, fears:

He is a male horse.

Money. It is so expensive to do this.

The risk of animal protestors boycotting the performance. Need to meet with the

and it is here that the predicament of the whole project itself becomes clear. We are making a performance that explores the light of Brighton, but how do you give *shape* to light? When do you know that you've even seen it when in fact you can't even 'isolate' it? The light just *is present*. The presence of Phoenix cuts through any sense of pretence and attempt at dramatic representation. Phoenix is a real encounter with – and direct experience of – something 'living', something that 'just is'. The horse does not *pretend* to be, nor does he have to work hard at 'not pretending'. Phoenix is not *acting* being a horse, he is one.

When the performers start moving around Phoenix we notice a change. They are humble, still and gentle as they discover what it means to be – and move – in the presence of an animal. We're learning from Phoenix. We discover a heightened, intense, gentle and real way of being. Everything orbits around the calm yet alert Phoenix. The performers need not 'invent' ideas or assert themselves in the space, they need not worry about what and how they communicate a certain idea. Rather, material emerges from their explorations of what it means to be and move with Phoenix.

Phoenix inspires a different way of perceiving and making. He is not a symbol of the light, but he does become the one thing in the space that reminds

RSPCA and the council's animal welfare officer.

The risk that he will one day refuse to walk down the stairs into the space. You can't force a ton of horse to walk down the stairs. We are vulnerable to the vagaries of his animal will. What happens if we have to perform without him?

But now that we've seen him, felt his heat, touched him: how can we do without him?

What does Phoenix do? He is a metaphor, an embodiment of light, of nature. And he is absolutely real. Not metaphor, only horse: his absolute horseness. It is the horseness, the real, which might make the performance possible. He arrests. He makes it clear than there is something unusual happening here. He indicates to the audience that this is not a theatre show, that we are in a different territory. He prepares people for the strange ambiguities of the piece. He is the strange ambiguity.

Rehearsals. Week three (we can't afford him for the first 3 weeks). We've made a wooden horse, to stand in for him, to help us get used to an obstacle where otherwise we'd get used to empty space. It's heavy and much less agile than the real thing. We start with a whole wooden horse. When we get tired of moving it around, we just move the front half. A long nose. A head, flank, front legs. A vertical line and a space where the rest of a horse should be.

Week four. We're still devising, still trying to work out the structure. I feel lost. The day he arrives: teach Phoenix where he needs to be and what he needs

us of the enormity of the natural phenomenon which we're exploring. His very presence prompts us to think differently about the material. Gilles Deleuze and Felix Guattari have proposed the notion of 'becoming-animal' when thinking about perception. To become animal does not mean that one acts or becomes *like* an animal. Rather it denotes the power, not to conquer what is other than the self, but to transform oneself in perceiving difference (Gilles Deleuze & Felix Guattari (1988): *A Thousand Plateaus*, London, Athlone, 243). Thus becoming-animal is also the process of being changed by something, to let something *expand* our perception. Colebrook suggests that instead of understanding the animal as a symbol (what does it mean or represent?), the animal is 'a possible opening for new styles of perception' (Claire Colebrook (2002): *Gilles Deleuze*, London, Routledge, 137). So it is with Phoenix: he opens up a different way of imagining the material, for us and hopefully for the audience. He does not symbolise the natural light of Brighton, but his presence becomes crucial for our exploration; it is as if his presence is a constant reminder of what is important, why and how.

His complete stillness is electric. He changes our behaviour in the space. Everything orbits around him.

JAMIE: Being with Phoenix often made me feel very emotional. Something about how rooted and immense he was. Sometimes if something went wrong I just focused on him and it brought me back to the moment.

to do in the performance. But we haven't made it yet. Kevin or Cindy on stage with him, often at the back of the space. I'm aware that they have dropped into a kind of surreal chaos. Images and noise and sound and abstract improvisations. Talking and microphones and a wind machine and strobes and a very big set. He can only just fit under the top of the middle frame. He doesn't feel like indifference. He feels like an obstacle. He feels like pressure. He feels like expectation, and I can't give anyone what he wants.

I talk to Kevin and Cindy, explain that we're not really ready, ask them to be patient. They understand. We continue devising. He comes in the afternoon. We fall into his rhythm, our breaks and schedules mapped onto the needs of a horse. The structure starts to appear. Jamie Bradley will be the one who is most closely connected to Phoenix, leading him when he needs to be led, improvising with him.

I remember Phoenix learned his cue. Every rehearsal, and then every night, when he hears the line that heralds his entrance, he starts to walk.

I remember there was a moment in the performance when he and Jamie come to the very front of the stage, and we wanted him to look out of the frame at the audience. His gaze, terrifying, intense.

In that moment time stopped, and here in the space is pure observation, pure being, pure presence. And then it's over and we carry on.

I remember someone was allergic. I remember sneezing. I remember we had a packet of antihistamines somewhere in case someone had an asthma attack.

We see things through him. It felt like he brought us closer together.

LAURA: He pulled us together as a group.

BETH: He made me feel small but not inconsequential, rather a part of a bigger environment. It was as if he tied everything together, and reminded you that it's alright to be still, and just to be.

JAMIE: I loved the moment every night when I left the stage to bring him on for the first time, and I was greeted by his neutral stare (not nervous, not excited) before stepping back into the piece.

He had an instinctive awareness of the audience and often turned his attention directly towards them.

LAURA: I remember the warmth coming off him. When you

I remember the fear every night that he wouldn't come down the ramp.

I remember the performances when he came onstage with his penis hanging out.

I remember we had a dustpan and brush and a mop and bucket at the back of the stage, in case we had to pause the performance to clear up after him.

I remember the people who walked out, angry that there was an animal in the piece.

I remember the moment when he appeared onstage, the reaction.

I remember, every night, grinning in the dark, as a white horse, ton of animal, heat and flesh, walked into the space.

I remember how he fell asleep during most performances, one hoof cocked, head bowed. I remember how sad that made him look. I remember his moods. Truculent sometimes. Playful sometimes. Alert sometimes. Bored sometimes. Asleep. Asleep a lot of the time.

Here we are, in The Basement. Mid performance. Over there, there is light, the frames set as a receding perspective. I hear music. Someone is speaking. The pluck of a double bass, and Jamie asks Laura, "What colour is the sky?"

And over there, towards the back, watching, ears pricked, listening, attracted by something Jamie McCarthy has played on the violin, part of this event but separate, listening, then disengaged, alert then asleep, here but elsewhere.

Here is a horse. A horse is here. A horse here is.

He just is.

David: The horse – a metaphor for the light. Indifferent, wild, beautiful nature, natural light. He is the ground on which we build our landscape. He will not be part of our 'art'. He is pure being. The horse exists in a different space and time from us. He stands, shifts his weight, lives in his body.

Around him, we make our attempts to say something about the light.

He just is.

got up close, about an inch around him was hot and smelled fantastic.

I remember an almighty thunder roll as he came down the ramp as were doing our pre-show warm up. And every time someone saying, "Phoenix is here."

I remember running to the toilet just before the performance started, shaking out my wrists and legs, and passing a horse.

I remember the surprise of a horse's head appearing out of the venue's doorway, every night, as he left.

JAMIE: I remember it didn't matter how many hours we'd rehearsed with him, or how far we'd got into the run, it was always a shock to see him standing in the dark corner, waiting.

LAURA: I felt young around him. I felt time around him. I felt potentiality around him.

He just is.

HORSE VISIT

1. Rehearsal / reaction / improvisation

2. Interaction: what can we discover new?

3. Horse's presence during other things

4. Filming

YES THINGS – his size
his stillness
his presence
his gaze
his first appearance

NO THINGS – aimless clippety clop
his big cock

> From: Kevin Smith > Date: 2 January 2008 22:37 > To: David Harradine > Subject: *RE next year* >
Hi David > Staying near Phoenix is only necessary because i've only quoted the diesel price from the stables and back again not extra travelling. also we would be in the lorry so parking would also be a problem. i dont think staying in a caravan is an option, 4 weeks is a long time in one. > we don't have another horse like Phoenix that's a mare. discussing the willy issue with Cindy she said when a horse is relaxed it's very possible that the willy will be extended not for sexual reasons just that he's relaxed, also when he goes for a wee he will extend his willy we simply can't do anything about this sorry. > We have a slight worry about the possibility of these animal protesters. we don't worry for ourselves or the safety of the horse it's just that if a few people start to make a noise or fuss when Phoenix is trying to go down the steps he just won't go down as he won't feel safe with a commotion going on behind him as you know from the last time we were down. as the entrance is on a main road we can't keep the public away like we could if we were on a film set, so i don't know what we can do about this as it's an unknown situation. > we also have to sort out where we are going to keep the lorry when we have dropped Phoenix off. > We will probably get the RSPCA involved if we go ahead as it's a good idea to get them on-side and also get their opinions. > Kevin

PHOENIX

---

very can't even begin to approach him

his extraordinary stillness. Calm. Solidy, grounded presence

when he looks at you he looks into your soul.

trying to imagine him and her remains absolutely indifferent.

member of the ensemble. He can be part of, he can

observe, be witness to, indifferent to, anything, everything.

is what he is : cock, shit, horse.

he, such capacity for extraordinary stillness. A living image.

moment of looking when I wonder if he's real. And then,

tiny moment; an ear, a snout, a foot. He's here.

can picture him in everything. He could just be. Being

a forest. A reminder of something other. Always present.

of this but separate; inside, but out, elsewhere.

moment, the end of the day. People moving, resting,

going up. He stands, absolutely still, absolutely just himself,

sit over there, a constant reminder, but also connecting

on becoming with to; I can look at others, at other

things, at the same time as being aware of him

This plan shows some of the ways in
which Phoenix's presence transformed
the basement.

1 Halfway through the
   performance he
   stopped here to look
   at the audience
2 He often fell asleep
   in this corner
3 Water
4 Hay
5 We kept a fan here
   to keep him cool
6 Horse's head poking
   out of door here

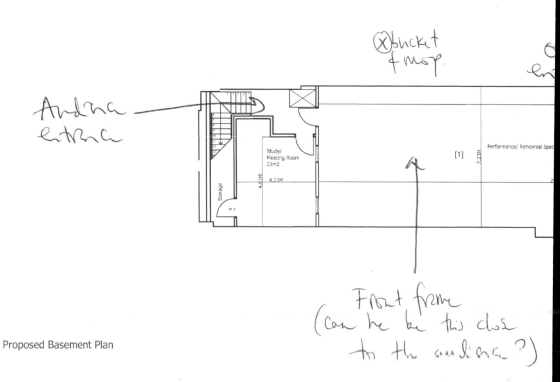

Proposed Basement Plan

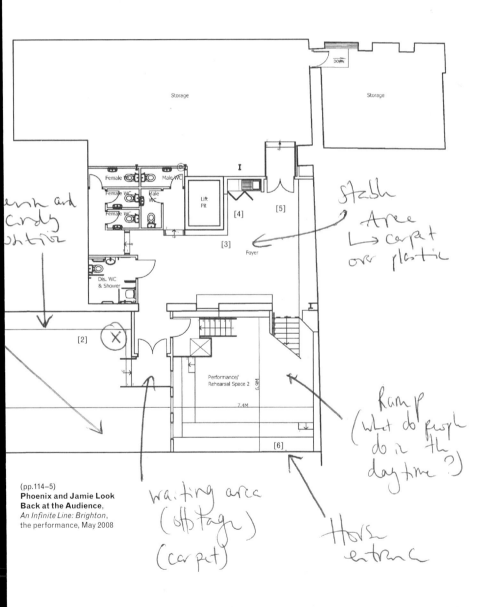

Storage

Storage

DOWN

Female Male WC

Female WC Male WC

Female WC

Lift Pit

[4] [5]

[3] Foyer

Dis. WC & Shower

[2] (X)

Performance/ Rehearsal Space 2

6.9M

7.4M

[6]

Stable Area ⌐→ carpet over plastic

Ramp (what do people do in the daytime?)

Horse entrance

waiting area (offstage) (carpet)

... and Cindy ...

(pp.114–5)
Phoenix and Jamie Look Back at the Audience,
An Infinite Line: Brighton,
the performance, May 2008

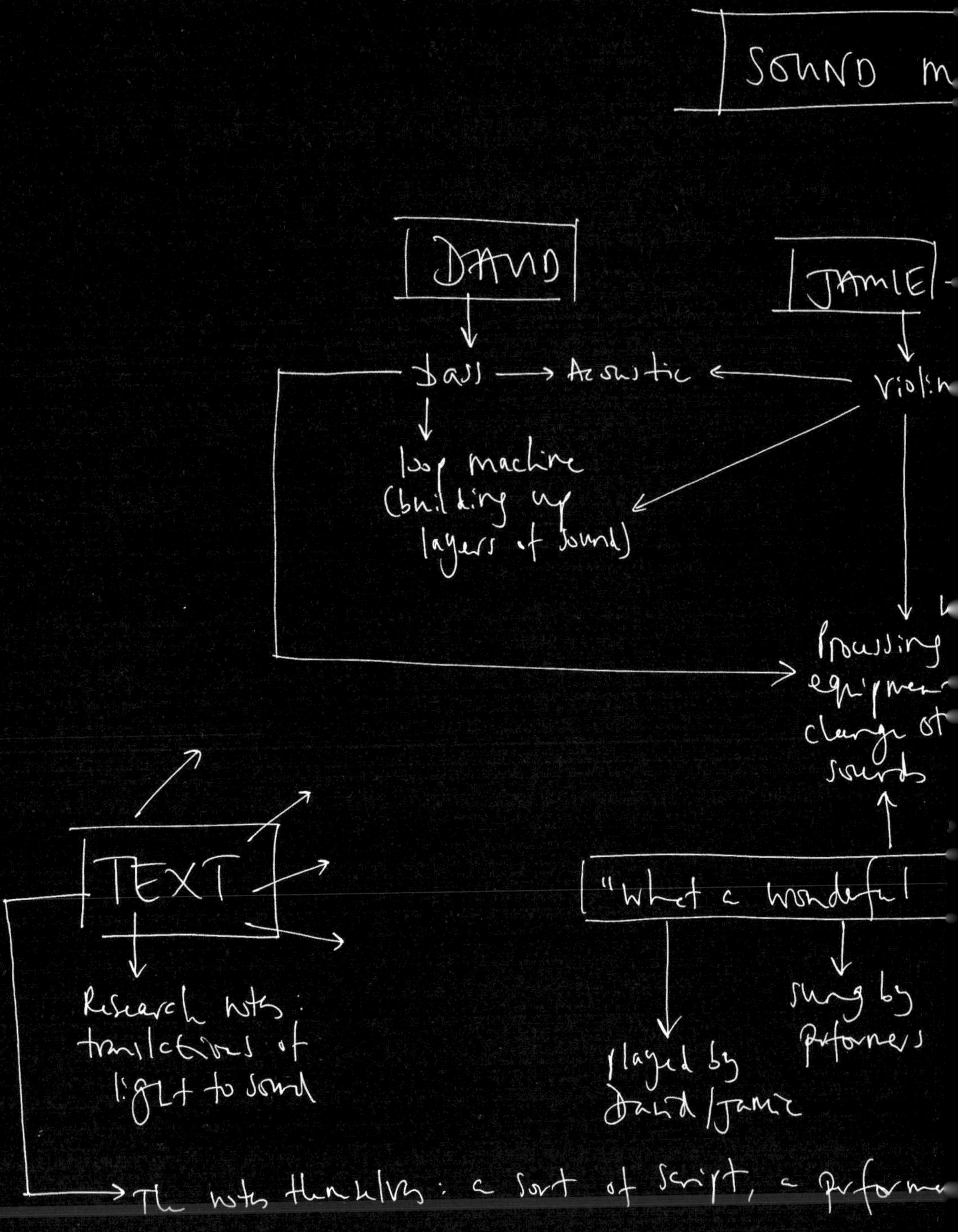

SOUND m

DAVID

JAMIE

bass → Acoustic ← violin

loop machine
(building up
layers of sound)

Processing
equipment
change of
sounds

TEXT

"What a wonderful

Research notes:
translations of
light to sound

played by
David/Jamie

sung by
performers

The notes themselves: a sort of script, a performa

... SOUND

**How did we generate sound and
music for the performance?**

During the year of research visits to
Brighton, one of the repeated questions
that provided a structure for observation
was, "What is the sound of the light?"
This question was a challenge: it
demanded that a silent visual phenomenon was imagined as sound, and that
this sound be described in words.

**WHAT IS THE SOUND
OF THE LIGHT?**

*"... a low buzz or hum,
muffled; an almost
ultrasonic whine
behind... like water, like
a river or the sea, only
thick: a golden gravy
river kind of sound...
a shimmering sound,
a low to medium pitch
hum, everywhere, from
all directions, a totally
non specific sound,
the sound of opacity...
a pure open tone, a kind
of cascade of sound,
descending... a finger
round a wine glass.
Pure. Fragile. Sustained
... a sine wave, mid
range, with a very
high, almost dog high,
piercing note above...
choral, a choir, but
distant, subtle...
a grinding, churning:
sand on the sea bed,
mixed with a smooth,
sexual sound... a quiet
sigh, a sad sigh...
a really piercing,
horrible, high pitched
siren. Unbearably loud
and sharp. But not
discordant... a dog
grumble, thin keen,
soft explosion..."*

Growing from the emphasis on sound in
this research, sound and music became
central to the development of material,
and the ways we created and worked
with sound and music were vital to the
rhythm of the devising, structuring and
presentation of the performance.

Instruments, Media, Forms

*Why did we work with the particular
sound sources we used?*

> The double bass: I had worked with
> David Leahy (double bass player)
> on several projects before
> *An Infinite Line: Brighton*, and I
> wanted him to work with us as a
> trusted collaborator who brought a
> great experience as an improviser/
> creator. There was no particular
> reason why the double bass itself
> was a significant sound for the
> project: it was simply the instrument
> that came with David.

> *The violin:* Jamie McCarthy had
> worked with David on another
> project which I'd seen, and I was
> interested in developing, through
> a different instrument, the string-
> based sound that I had been
> exploring with David. Jamie joined
> us for the initial R&D, to see if there
> was a place for the violin in the
> sound world of the project, and to

[115]

see if we wanted to work together. As well as playing the violin, Jamie does a lot of vocal work, and would often sing, or vocalise, during improvisations. His playing has an emotional intensity that felt really right for the experiential aspects of the project, so much of which was about the *feeling* of encountering the light. We decided to work together.

The electronics: The descriptions that came out of the research visits frequently suggested sounds that were clearly not those made by a string instrument, and so I really wanted to explore electronic sound, and to work with a sound artist who could create digital sound and explore live processing of the sounds the other performers made in the piece. Mark brought these things.

Recorded song: In my own thinking about how to approach the project, I had been considering the light in Brighton as being constant and yet endlessly different from itself – characterised by similarity and change. I had an idea to explore this sonically, through the use of a repeated song, so I bought nine different versions of Louis Armstrong singing 'What a Wonderful World'. Why this song? Partly the lyric, with its reference to landscape (trees, clouds, the sky of blue) but mainly as it's so iconic, a song that everyone recognises: familiar enough for people to be able to hear when we were using different versions.

So these were our raw materials:

a set of descriptions of the sound of the light;

a double bass;

a violin;

voice;

electronic sounds;

processing equipment;

Louis Armstrong singing 'What a Wonderful World';

and of course the text, the voices of the performers, the sound of the projectors, the sound of the space.

Generating Material

Before rehearsals, Mark spent some time taking the descriptions from the research visits, and composing sound pieces that he felt represented these descriptions in sonic form. It was very useful to have these pre-composed files in the rehearsal room, and Mark would often suggest ways of integrating them into the material, or using them to add further texture or layers to music that was being created live. Later, when we were structuring material, and trying different combinations of things in quick succession, I had to find a language for remembering all the different sound files, as I couldn't remember the difference between the sounds indicated by Mark's number-and-letter based names *(fig. 1)*

Throughout all the stages of improvisation, sound was a key part of what we created, and I would ask Jamie and David to respond to stimuli musically, in the same way that I was asking Jamie

SOUND FILES - Descriptions

P101   High, fluttershimmer, cicada, flvrr
P1011   Cave of bats, drips, vinyl crackle
P11   Space shimmerhum, drill, pierce, synth
P3   Dog high, piercing pitch
P41   mid + high metal knocking, stab, brrrzzz, drill, jazzy tap
P411   Hooverishock wind, shimmerthrough
P5   Dog grunsh, explosion   SET SHIFTS / OPENING
P6   Burring doghigh flutter pulse, mid whrrr

F1_SD   Gremlin windrush pixie Lois's
F2_SD   Radio untuned pixie Lois's into windflutterrush
F4_SD   Crushedsuck Lois's [towards end?]
H1_SD   Earthintrudersmarchingchoir rewind Lois's
H2_SD   Fastbackwards squeezed Lois's
H4_SD   Speedup pitch shift helium scale Lois's

SHKPV2   Beautiful trapped loop ✱ Start?
↯SHKS1   Alien blipper squeak — maybe?
SHKS3   Electricshimmer space tube ✱ Start?
SHKS 4   Flattened patter shimmer with knocking
SHKS 5   Another flattened space shimmer + knocking

Ps (light sounds): any of these

Fs, Hs : probably too pixelated, too digital?

SHs : beginnings are good — prob. not vocal parts

(remember Jamie's "zithermist" CD track)

Bradley and Laura to respond through movement or text. Improvising music in response to light, to a material (chalk, water, mist), in response to colour, or in response to the responses of the other performers led to the creation of a huge amount of sonic material. The further we got into the process, the more we were able to refine these initial improvisations into more developed pieces. What might have started as a response to the rhythm of a projected image ("Can you play the rhythm of the flickering light of this projector?") later emerged as something more complex ("Jamie, can you play the movement of the seagull in this projection; David, can you play the changing colour of the sky the seagull's flying in?").

We talked a lot about who was leading – whether the musicians were following the improvisations of the performers, or whether the performers (Laura and Jamie) were moving in response to the music. Both these approaches led to the discovery of different sorts of ideas. At times I would ask just David to play, at others just Jamie, at others both. Sometimes Mark fed the material they were creating into his processing equipment, and that took things in a different direction.

They key thing in all of this was that sound and music were given a particular kind of presence in the process: rather than sonic material being composed outside the rehearsal room, we worked in a way that caused sound to emerge alongside everything else, in a fluid way, in a responsive way, in a way that could be fleet-footed and that could change and develop alongside the changing and development of other things.

Later in the process this brought its own problems, as what we didn't have time for was a period of refinement in the sound, through which specifically musical concerns such as progression and compositional development could be addressed. In an ideal world we would have had more time, and would have allowed time specifically to develop the sound and music in this way.

Translation

One of key ways we generated sound was through an idea of translation, all based in improvised responses to different kinds of stimuli, following different instructions:

> **Play in response to a particular light.**

> **Play in response to the movement of another performer.**

> **Take an image from the text, and translate this into sound:** for example, an image of sitting on the beach over the course of a day. I asked David to explore and create the sound of the rising and falling tides; Jamie to make the sound of the sun arcing over the sky; Mark to think about the other sound and noise in the city: the traffic, the seagulls, the people on the pier.

> **Play the words of the text as music.**

> **Research the frequency of the colours described in the text and explore these through frequencies of sound.**

> **Make a recording of spoken words and build them up into layers and compositions that transform the language into music. Explore different ways of doing that.**

August 07 R&D:
David, Synne and Mark

The list of possible examples here is endless: what's key is that sound and music were usually generated through responses to challenges or questions or images. As with the physical improvisations, we were never looking for something that was 'right' as in being correct – sound doesn't work in that definitive a way – but rather we tried to *create motivations for generating material*. In providing these stimuli, I would sometimes ask questions that I knew to be impossibly hard to answer ("Can you make the sound of the dark space at the far side of the night sky?"),

not out of some perverse will to make the task impossible, but because impossible requests can bring a kind of release: with the knowledge that it's impossible to achieve something, we recognise that any response is equally valid, and that brings liberation and a willingness to try anything and to respond from a place of instinct rather than a place of rationality and thought.

Throughout these periods of creation and experimentation, when we heard material that excited us, we made a note of how we'd made it and added it to a list of discoveries that we might come back to and use later, once we knew more about the contexts in which it might appear.

Atmosphere

In the end the performance felt, more than anything else, like a progression of images which unfolded in a dense and rich sound universe: the sound and music provided a sort of glue or cement which bound together fragmented visual, textual and physical material. The piece was rarely silent, only momentarily pausing between sections before a new sound emerged to signal the start of something else. The sound and music provided emotional and sensual texture. It was often through the use of sound that an ambiguous image became more concrete, giving the audience a clearer sense of our intention, of how we hoped the image might engage the viewer.

Sound and Structure

The sound also became vital in working out the structure of the piece. We worked with sound in a number of structural ways:

> **As a source of energy.**

Arriving at the end of one section, and needing to find a way to move into the next, we found that sound often gave the necessary impulse. The electronic sounds were particularly vital in this, as they often had a harshness and a sharp-edged quality that acted like a jolt or electric shock. They would push us forward.

> **As a transition.**

Sound also functioned as a bridge between sections. When the set was being reconfigured or during the preparation or dismantling of an image, music and sound could bloom and come into focus, in ways that filled the spaces where momentum and rhythm could have been lost.

> **As a structural motif.**

We worked a lot with repetition in the sound: the reoccurrence of 'What a Wonderful World'; the use of one of Mark's compositions (his response to my description of the light as a 'dog grumble') as an indicator that there would be a major set reconfiguration.

> **As a cue.**

In a complex piece where any one moment might involve the appearance of a light, the movement of a performer, the initiation of an action, or the emergence of a new sound, we found that following sound itself was often the best way of bringing things together; following sound as the initiator of a new thing or the next

moment; sound being the thing that told us when something was about to happen.

The sound and music in *An Infinite Line: Brighton* worked in many other complex ways. It allowed us to explore ideas of landscape and chaos that developed into guiding concepts; it could foreground the important idea of material emerging 'in the present moment'; it often functioned as a way of fore-grounding the passing of time.[1]

[1] There's more on these ideas in the chapter **Discovering Concepts**, Inventing a Language.

OTHER THINGS

- text / voice
- Sound of the
        projectors
- wineglass + water
- wind machine
- Phoenix's hooves

Pre-made
electronics

MARK

LiVe voice
Tape recorded
megaphone
microphone
Processed

→ played through PA

...cording played on stage

... words as sound.

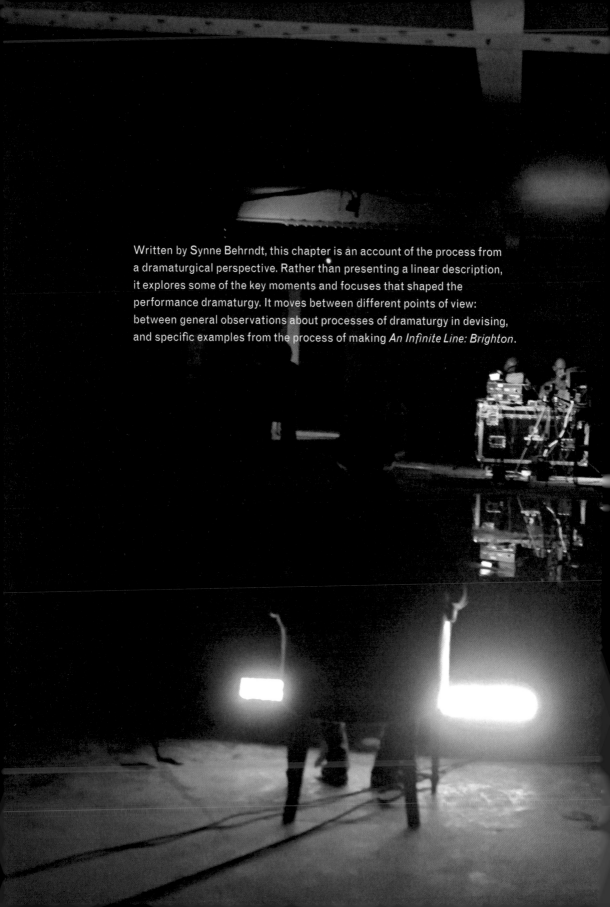

Written by Synne Behrndt, this chapter is an account of the process from
a dramaturgical perspective. Rather than presenting a linear description,
it explores some of the key moments and focuses that shaped the
performance dramaturgy. It moves between different points of view:
between general observations about processes of dramaturgy in devising,
and specific examples from the process of making *An Infinite Line: Brighton*.

Shaping a Dramaturgy [122–143]

1 WHAT DOES IT MEAN TO THINK DRAMATURGICALLY ABOUT THE PROCESS?

When we discuss how we created *An Infinite Line: Brighton*'s performance dramaturgy we can try and draw a linear time line that maps how and why decisions were made. After all, there was a chain of events that led to a final performance and structure. However, when we try and piece together these events we begin to realise that the story of how the performance came together is far from linear. Rather, information, ideas and solutions arrived at different stages and in different guises, and often solutions that seemingly revealed themselves at a later stage turned out to have been with us all the time. One could describe the timeline of our devising process as circular: the more material we accumulated the more we were in fact revisiting and expanding the same ideas. Throughout the process there was a quiet insistence to pursue something and to return to ideas in order to find out what they could reveal. One such example is the way in which *What a Wonderful World* became a shared obsession. We would always look for opportunities to introduce and weave this song, or its echoes and residues, into the material.

The dramaturgical task was not to write a story, rather the intention was to help flesh out and articulate a precise conceptual space that the work could inhabit, and then to work out the kinds of rules and ideas that govern this space. It was about being present, watching, waiting and then trying to describe and articulate what had revealed itself. It was about being alert to what was happening in the space and to be as precise as possible about what I saw and experienced, in order to work out what was important in the work, and then to help shape and distil the material into a structure. It was also about working out *what* the piece could be about (content) as well as *how* it was (structure and form). In short, it was about observing, distilling and organising patterns, and finding ways of extracting an emotional as well as conceptual content.

At the early stages of the process I tried to gain an *overview* of the emerging ideas by naming and organising the material. This process of naming the moments that emerged from the practical improvisations was essentially a way to articulate as precisely as possible the potential of what could seem like a vague hunch or an emerging and embryonic idea. It could also be a way to try and explain and name a certain feeling or atmosphere in the space, as well as a means of grasping and remembering what was going on in the improvisations. After our first two R&D weeks I organised the material into fifteen different 'threads' or 'strands':

[1] The sea and light [2] Recreation attempts [3] A sense of mystery [4] The body's response to light/climate/weather [5] Ghosts, past/ memory [6] A sense of discovering and following in the footsteps of someone else's experience [7] The challenge of translating/ transformation [8] To 'narrate' light [9] Different times/different places [10] Something is revealed [11] A chain of responses – the ensemble [12] Real time/real effort [13] Different levels of reality [14] Hide and seek [15] Direct experience – the force of nature (Phoenix – the horse)

I was essentially beginning to shape a 'road map' for a dramaturgy in that I was looking for similarities and potential connections and relationships between the different threads. Whilst I was becoming clearer about the different ideas, patterns and structures that were emerging I would also try and articulate the overarching idea or concept that could *connect* them. Initially I extracted three key ideas that connected the fifteen threads: 'process'; 'search'; 'immersion'. However, at the early stage of the process it was also important to resist the temptation to force connections too soon. It was important to not fix the material, or limit the possible directions that the work could take. It was important to allow the material to mature. The challenge was to be precise without narrowing possibilities, to be open without being too vague or unhelpfully abstract. What was equally important, however, was that material was not lost, forgotten or ignored.

2 TOWARDS A DRAMATURGY

In one sense when I look for patterns, I observe how actions and textures in the space are beginning to take shape and organise themselves into more tangible ideas. No thing is insignificant, rather I look for material in every little thing as we try to work out how an emerging spatial or physical pattern, a micro event, an interaction between two performers, or even a particular spatial dynamic or sonic quality could have the potential to be expanded. One could say that I am on the lookout for dramaturgical 'hooks'. By 'hook' I mean something that gives you a way into the material. It may be something that keeps appearing in the material, and the more often 'it' reappears the more you begin to understand that it could be a 'hook'. This initial hook could then become a narrative driver in the work. By this I mean that a recurring idea could be expanded into a form of narrative thread that runs through the performance as a whole. To give an example, in the extended improvisations I noticed a particular atmosphere where time and space expanded yet at the same time felt compressed. This particular atmosphere was difficult to name or pin down, but it had to do with the way in which the lengthy improvisations enabled the performers to improvise actions, which they would embroider and layer ad infinitum. The improvisations would leave the air thick with real exhaustion and a sense of lingering melancholy, stillness and contemplation. Often these improvisations would end with the performers joining each other in an ensemble-choreography, as if they would naturally gravitate towards each other when they felt that the time was right, and when they felt that they had exhausted all possibilities. The (slow) duration created a sense of actual and real struggle or effort. The performers were not acting or pretending to be exhausted, they were not pretending to be watching each other carrying out tasks, rather they were genuinely exploring the moment – and they were genuinely exhausted from doing so. I also noticed that at times the performers seemed lost in the activity as if they were *searching* for something, seemingly unsure about the next move, and yet also intent on being immersed in the task at hand. During an improvisation in our R&D labs in January 2008 this was very pronounced, and in my dramaturgical notes I have underlined the question, "can we derive a spatial and choreographic principle from the performers adapting and adopting each other's actions and becoming gradually immersed in a group activity?" There was a strong sense of intuitive and instinctive intelligence, and I kept imagining them as animals moving together towards a shared goal. The image of animals admittedly came to me because of Phoenix, knowing that he may be in the performance, but I also found that the performers' quiet movement and very intuitive way with each other in the space reminded me of the way in which animals move with and around each other.

The choreographic principle that emerged from the performers' improvisations could be organised into a five-step structure:

[1] Observing each other [2] Adapting to other people's actions
[3] Adopting actions [4] Inhabiting the action [5] Just being
(completely immersed).

It was here that I also became more interested in the notion of 'togetherness' and the 'ensemble' itself. I wondered if we could make the ensemble and their sense of togetherness the content for the performance. Could their process, joint struggle as well as shared joy when trying to re-create the light be the thing that would drive the structure forward and join together the different images and actions? Could this perhaps be a narrative driver in the performance?

This narrative driver, which I named the *joint effort to explore the process of making something happen*, revealed itself in the material repeatedly. In an early R&D session this sense of searching together revealed itself when Jamie McCarthy, Mark, and David Leahy were intensely focused on creating different instrumental versions of *What a Wonderful World*. Here the search became about Jamie, Mark and David trying to find a particular sound or perhaps an essence in the song. It was also about a group of people working together to create *something*. During another improvisation Jamie, Mark and David tried to translate David's colour descriptions into sound, and their joint effort to find the right sound with any (musical) means possible was compelling to watch. At first their actions would seem random or haphazard, yet as the improvisations went on there was a distinct sense that they were in fact *preparing* for *something*. It occurred to me that what looked like musicians setting up equipment *was* in fact an exploration of sound. They were looking for sound in everything, in the tuning of an instrument, or the ways in which an object, the space or the phonetics of certain words could produce sound. Again I detected the potential of *ensemble*, *live exploration* and *process* as performance aesthetics and dramaturgy. I would soon start to look consciously for how these ideas were manifest in everything we did. It became interesting to see in how many ways this notion of the ensemble and pursuit of light would appear in the material, and soon everything that happened in the space could potentially feed this narrative, including the way in which (on some occasions) the performers would interrupt an improvisation and ask if they could begin again, or profess that they found some descriptions of light impossible to 'perform'. I started to collect these moments, and began to feel like a detective who was looking for more evidence to support a case. These ideas were initially hooks that gave us something to work from and with, and they provided something tangible to hold onto in the improvisations. But I also had to ask myself if I was becoming fixated on the same ideas, and if this meant that I was leaving out other important possibilities. Yet at what point in the process would it be necessary to make decisions and to start editing the material? My discussions with David were about many things, but in terms of my dilemma they were moments that brought me back to the crucial question, "what does the material 'speak of' in terms of light and in particular the light of Brighton?" This question gave me a lateral yet structured way of responding to the material and to become clear about the whys and hows of our decisions.

The notion of 'the search' as well as the struggle to translate the ephemeral light into language is a strong theme in David's notes from the year of research visits. I observed that the text maps a journey of impressions and descriptions over the course of a year as a roaming 'flâneur of light' attempts to capture light in different geographical places in Brighton. The research notes invoke a sense of restless movement as the observer's eye moves like a roaming camera from place to place and captures snapshots of Brighton's light. The light, however, remains difficult to encapsulate, and there is a prevailing feeling that it is futile to try to represent or be completely precise about it. As David remarks in the notes, there is 'no accuracy, just impression'. The notes' prevailing feeling of a persistent pursuit of accuracy whilst knowing that there can only be impression, or interpretation, was echoed in the performers' genuine struggle to 'translate' or 'perform' the descriptions of light. At the same time I observed that they would challenge each other to carry out more and more difficult translation tasks. They were aware that they were just playing a game.

The improvisations revealed another interesting pattern where the performers would oscillate between what I would name concrete space/time and poetic space/time: we began with simple tasks and gradually an action would expand from a pedestrian or prosaic action into a poetic or abstracted moment or tableau. Once this poetic moment had settled the performers would dismantle it and return to the concrete reality of the 'here and now'. As David put it, we were creating dramatic, theatrical and poetic images whilst reminding the audience that the performance was "really just a group of people in a space doing something together with a lot of stuff." This confirmed that the performance would be about an ensemble in pursuit of (re)creating light, and that they would challenge each other to find the most creative ways in which to translate *descriptions* of light into practice and performance. They were an ensemble *driven* forwards by an endless pursuit of the perfect recreation attempt or challenge. More poetically speaking one could say that they were also abstract and instinctual bodies that were driven like moths towards the light, their journey ending with the brightest of lights.

Our use of the research notes informed dramaturgical decisions in that the performers' attempt to reconstruct David's own journey meant that their pursuit could also be interpreted as a mapping of or attempt at recreating someone else's experience. The creative team were essentially following in David's footsteps, and thus we were trying to understand his relationship to Brighton's light. This premise led to the use of headphones in the performance: whenever the performers spoke extracts from the notes they put on headphones to listen to David's voice and words. The headphones enabled us to sign post, or gesture towards, the ideas of re-creation and re-tracing a journey.

3 THE BEATING HEART

At every stage of the process there were moments that shifted or confirmed my understanding of the piece significantly, and it seemed important to keep a balance between keeping things open and knowing that decisions had to be made. As I discussed earlier, I was often faced with this dilemma, and I had to remind myself to take a step back and look for other possible 'drivers'. It paradoxically became very important to be able to *doubt* productively, and I became interested in those moments that produced a shared feeling or understanding between everyone in the rehearsal space. We can make decisions about material conceptually after lengthy conversations, but there were those moments during our improvisations where everybody in the room recognised that we had discovered something that felt like the central core or 'heart' of the performance. These moments are crucial because they enable the entire ensemble and company to recognise what the performance is about, and they give a vital clue as to what may be holding together the overall dramaturgy. I would not have discovered these moments had I not been in the space with the company during *all* rehearsals, and my task was to find a way to articulate and name why and how something was the beating heart of the structure and performance.

One such 'beating heart' moment was Laura's 'Roedean dance'. Laura started dancing and did not stop until she had exhausted herself. The other performers watched quietly, as if they knew that she could and should not be stopped. We recognised that her dance encapsulated the sense of relentless pursuit. We knew that Laura's dance summed up the entire performance: it was the central image or action which joined together different themes or ideas.

There were other crucial moments where everyone knew that an important discovery had been made, such as when we discovered the cue or impulse for the set reconfigurations and transitions. Mark's 'Dog Grumble' sound underscored the transitions, and it gave the performers a sonic instruction to reconfigure the set. The change of the set marked the transition between the episodes, and this sound gave the transitions an impulse and intention. The sound did not provide a psychological explanation for why the performers were reconfiguring or moving the set, rather it could be interpreted as a subliminal impulse that would drive the performers forward. There would later be other reasons why scenes changed, yet the 'Dog Grumble' with its driving and industrial jarring sound, taken together with the performers' precise actions, inspired a way of thinking about the dramaturgy in terms of an unstoppable, relentless, inevitable and forward driving journey.

4 STRUCTURE

A crucial dramaturgical task is to devise a structure for the material, or to offer different perspectives on what the structure could be. Much time was spent devising structural possibilities, choreographic or spatial guidelines, and rules that could help give the material a shape or form. At the beginning of the process I used somewhat descriptive categories to organise the material, however as we developed a more fluid and creative language (for example 'landscape' and 'visual poem') our ideas for structure also started to develop. We became interested in an organic structure (such as a weather system) with its erratic ebbs and flows that we often observed in the improvisations, but we soon realised that the structural quality that we were after could not be improvised in the performance, rather it had to be meticulously recreated. We also became aware that although we had not devised a linear story, it was helpful to think of the performance as a journey where the performers had an explicit project. Their project was to look for light and the sun until they had exhausted themselves. Thus the structure consisted of a series of episodes that were held together by the notion of a forward moving journey that began at sunrise and ended at the moment when the sun is at its highest. The final image could be interpreted as a moment of arrival, as if to suggest that the journey had come to an end. Although there was a journey in that we moved forward in time and there was even a climax (Laura's Roedean dance), the structure could also be interpreted as circular in that the same pattern but with different actions was repeated throughout. The overall structure consisted of a series of micro-structures or individual episodes that followed the same compositional and dramaturgical principle: the performers would gradually build a moment or 'attempt', and when this moment had reached a climax, or its final shape, they would disband and collapse it, move on to the next moment and attempt, and the same process would start again. This gave the impression of repetition, although in fact the structure was moving towards a resolution. This sense of repetition linked to David's observation that the weather and light are erratic and changeable yet at the same time also constant and continuous. There was thus an interesting tension between difference, repetition and sameness.

Perhaps somewhat paradoxically it was the question about how to be precise when grappling with abstract and fluid ideas and concepts that also made us gravitate towards a poetic language. As discussed in the chapter *Discovering Concepts, Inventing a Language* this enabled us to develop a conceptual space for the work, and with this shift in (or discovery of) terminology we were also able to imagine and speak about the material and composition from a sensorial, temporal and spatial perspective. The notion of landscape and visual poetry felt opening and generative. We imagined the performance as a living ecosystem in which the elements were forever trying to find equilibrium between order and chaos. It enabled us think of the structure in terms of a rhythmic and dynamic organism with its own rules and organisational logic. We became interested in the ways in which the seemingly temperamental, forever shifting nature of the weather and light could translate into a structure and a dramatic world that is governed by a natural system's movement towards equilibrium. Although the general pace and rhythm of the performance was partly slow and durational, like a vast landscape, the notion of erratic weather systems also informed the way in which the changes between the episodes and the rhythm and pace of the individual episodes manifested themselves in terms of sudden interruptions and abrupt endings, and with the slowness often followed by short and explosive bursts.

To conceive of the project as 'not a theatre piece' prompted us to approach the material and process *sideways*, so to speak, and this meant looking for the conceptual ideas as well as emotional content embedded in our starting point. Our discussions about light and the ways in which it affects behaviour inadvertently moved on to ideas about experiential processes, perception and the way in which human beings live and exist within an ecosystem and natural landscape. We became interested in what it meant to try not to disturb or control, rather to really be present *with something*, for example the landscape and light. We used the metaphor of landscape to suggest a number of things, for example the open-ended and perhaps 'slower' mode of perception that is needed when searching for the light. The light is everywhere and yet no-where, and in order to really see it we have to pay attention to the smallest changes, details and nuances.

We have to be patient, wait and watch. Really watch. The performance attempted to engage an audience in the challenges of this process, and an important question was therefore how one might invite an audience to suspend their expectation of a linear narrative, and how one could invite them to really look, wait and watch and thereby engage with slow perceptual processes.

In her response to the performance, writer Cathy Turner contemplates the way in which it challenged the audience to engage in a viewing experience that did not place the performers, or perhaps the human being, at the centre. She remarked:

> Maybe the performers aren't at the centre. Maybe they are trying to point beyond themselves. That's really, really interesting and important. But it is also very difficult, because it breaks with all our viewing habits and our rush to identify and to place the human at the centre. I don't know if you can even do it. But you had a good go. There's a pointing beyond the performers, beyond the dark basement, to the non-human that surrounds us. Politically, I think that is hugely important and it connects to some of the turn towards landscape and space that I think we are seeing in performance right now.

Email correspondence with Cathy Turner, 19th May 2008.

Cathy Turner's point about the performers not being at the centre is crucial: the work was to a great extent about our relationship to our environment. David's research notes had many references to the relationship between weather, landscape and an emotional state, and there are several moments when the weather shapes the 'narrator' or observer's mood. There is a sense that the observer is not merely observing the weather and the landscape, rather that he begins to take on its characteristics. We became interested in the ways in which the human being became less of an observing outsider who 'studies' nature and the light and more a co-existing presence. Phoenix, the horse, was a radical and crucial dramaturgical intervention that distilled the relationship between human, nature and light into a direct, sensorial experience.

5 CONTENT – DISTILLING NARRATIVE DRIVERS

Devising processes create their own particular set of circumstances and conditions that inadvertently play a crucial role in how the structure and content are shaped. This is particularly evident when we reflect on the ways in which the ensemble's meeting with the conceptual and practical challenges of the topic shape the final performance structure.

The performance *An Infinite Line: Brighton* was about many things, but if we were to distil the question of content into a dramaturgical premise the performance was initially an exploration of Brighton's light, yet more specifically it became about the process of searching, and thus it was about watching and about keeping going in the hope of finding; about looking without being quite sure what one is looking for. It was a performance about waiting for something to reveal itself, and the joy that one experiences when something eventually emerges and one can – at least momentarily – grab hold of it. Much like the creative processes of devising and other artistic practices, it was a performance that explored how one makes sense of the inexplicable, and how one gives the intangible a form and shape. We were essentially faced with one of the oldest themes and challenges in art's practice, where the artist is moved to give artistic shape to (their feelings about) nature – and light.

Moreover, as David remarked at the outset of the rehearsals, it was important to keep in mind that the light essentially already says what needs to be said, so the task of the performance could be to try and embody the human experience of nature and light, to attempt to put this experience and feeling into words, sound, image, music and movement. One could say that the performance sought to embody or explore the very impossibility of making a performance *about* the light.

*check with Ali about pro?

Day	Time	What
MONDAY	9.30-10.45	warm up — (time alone physical / trames / m Rhythm n voice?
	10.45-1.15	Devising + Rehea
	1.15-2.30	DINNER
	2.30-3	Warm up / pcy / gan
	3-6	Devising / Rehearse
THES ⟶		pm non-tech re
WEDS	5pm	finish early for
17th		
FRI		
SAT SUN	} Additional tech time

EVENINGS??

What days will
Sophie be in .

... PROCESS

How did we structure and organise the creative process?

Covering research and development and, later, devising and rehearsals, the process through which we made the performance was broken down into several phases. This allowed us to explore particular ideas at particular points in the development of the project, and to step back from those explorations with time to reflect on what we'd discovered before we entered the next stage. Not including the initial research, which predated the devising process by two years, we conducted these intermittent creative and practical experiments over a twelve-month period:

> **Phase 1, April – August 2007**

Preliminary design ideas and preparation for the first stage of practical R&D; visiting suppliers and manufacturers of lighting equipment; working with the festival to confirm the performance space/site; making decisions on the creative team; considering various options on an animal's presence; developing working production budgets.

> **Phase 2, August 2007**

Two weeks full time practical R&D on site in The Basement, working with full creative team, with elements of lighting, sound, film and design.

> **Phase 3, August – December 2007**

Ongoing meetings and creative conversations, with various focuses: design/lighting development; dramaturgical/ conceptual development; decisions on casting and on working with a horse; developing and detailing production budgets; ongoing visits to Brighton to record cine films for installation and performance.

> **Phase 4, December 2007**

Practical 'laboratories' with a specific focus on the use of the text from the research visits as a starting point for generating sound.

> **Phase 5, January 2008**

  Practical laboratories focusing on translating the research text into movement.

> **Phase 6, January 2008**

  Practical laboratories focusing on ways of speaking and performing the research text as a sort of script.

> **Phase 7, January – March 2008**

  Finalising design ideas, commissioning set construction, finalising lighting and sound technology decisions and purchasing equipment as necessary; ongoing cine filming and purchase of cine projectors; ongoing work on production budgets.

> **Phase 8, April 2008**

  Four-week devising and rehearsal period.

What this timeline doesn't show are all the other practical and producing considerations and conversations that were taking place throughout this period, which were vital in order for the creative work to happen:

  ongoing fundraising; contracting the team;

  booking accommodation and travel;

  negotiation and contracting with the festival and venue;

  working with a press/PR agent to ensure publicity;

  managing the overall budget, and so on.

A typical week or a typical day during the periods of creative work would be structured differently depending on the particular focus of the work. For example, for the sound-focused labs we didn't spend as much time as we normally would doing physical warm ups, but we spent much more time than usual running very long improvisations, as there was a single focus (sound) rather than many focuses (sound, movement, text, image, etc).

During devising and rehearsals we started with a daily structure that we pretty much managed to maintain throughout:

The morning warm up was one of the most important parts of the day, and it developed a fixed structure:

> **About 10 minutes for everyone to do whatever they wanted, which tended to involve making a cup of tea and doing some stretches.**

> **About 20 minutes for either yoga or musical warming up. We had various pieces of equipment: yoga mats, a gym ball, a skipping rope, tennis balls, a football.**

> **About 15 minutes for ensemble work – rhythm exercises, group complicite work.**

> **About 15 minutes when everyone came together and played a game.**

(8–9.30): (Preparatory production & design work as necessary. This didn't happen every day);

9.30: Morning call for full team to arrive at the space;

9.30–10.30: Warm up;

10.45–1.30: Devising and/or rehearsals, with at least one 20 minute break;

1.30–2.45: Dinner break;

2.45–3.15: Warm up, games, preparation of the space to start working;

3.15–6: Devising and/or rehearsals, with at least one break;

After 6: Meetings, planning, tech & design work as necessary.

....

The after-dinner warm up was really just a very shortened version of this, normally involving a bit of rhythm work and then a game. We had the luxury of a separate studio for warm ups, which meant that all our personal belongings and the equipment we needed for our games and physical work was not in the devising/performance space: this separation was really useful in helping us focus on the different parts of the day: the preparatory parts and the creating parts and the taking-a-break-from-it parts. If we got stuck it was really beneficial to be able to leave the rehearsal room and go somewhere else for a game or a stretch. Having separate spaces where we would make tea and take breaks – and remembering to get up out of the basement and into the daylight – were also really important for ensuring our wellbeing.

The overall rehearsal schedule for the final devising period (the one leading up to performances) started as a fairly precisely planned structure. There were specific sessions when we knew we wouldn't be able to work technically (in order for Ali to have some time away from the rehearsal space to do other planning work). There were sessions in which we would focus specifically on light, or on working with the set and objects, or on sound. The patterns of these sessions were repeated across the first three weeks, so that it felt like we'd taken control of a complicated process.

Regular meetings were scheduled in:

> production meetings,
>
> design meetings,
>
> dramaturgy meetings.

The rhythm of the final week was altered by the arrival of Phoenix, the horse, and we had to always work to a schedule that gave him regular breaks and that meant he wasn't inside for more than 6 hours. In this final week there was the inevitable shift of focus onto preparing for the first performance (even though we were still devising and working on structure), with more time dedicated to finessing technical things – such as lighting, and film, and the choreography of objects, and sound.

Once we were into the performance period, our daily rhythm and structure shifted again, with time scheduled for us to meet before the pre-show warm up to talk about the previous show, and for us to make changes, or for me to give notes. These times felt like an extension of the devising and rehearsals, and it's undoubtedly the case that we all found it challenging to maintain the openness of searching that comes with devising at the same time as mustering the particular sort of energy it takes to perform.

The reality of the process, and the unexpected ways of working which it brought to light and demanded, inevitably meant that we didn't stick to this schedule rigidly – it adapted when it needed to – but it did provide us with a starting point, and a framework for structuring our daily activity. It also acted as a reminder, of how much time we had left – it structured the month of devising and rehearsals – and kept us mindful of what the important deadlines were (e.g. when we were supposed to have stopped devising; when we had to spend time focusing on technical refinement of the lighting and sound; when we had to make final decisions on the colour we wanted to paint the set; when Phoenix would be joining us).

The very act of sitting down and talking through and putting together the schedule meant that we had to consider in advance the key moments in the process, and *that* process – of talking and planning – was vital in giving ourselves a clear framework for trying to achieve what we had gone to Brighton to do.

~ meetings *

sal schedule draft 1

Notes

David / Jamie lead rhythm?

Jamie / Laura lead yoga (or David)

When will there be a break?
Does it need scheduling?

What does Ali need here?

Ali out of span

dir meeting

Jazz

Print a separate
copy with a
column for

personal staff-

meetings?

This chapter, which takes the form of a dialogue recorded a year after the project ended, explores some of the conceptual frameworks we created during the development and devising of the performance. It covers ideas around poetry, weather and landscape, and considers some of the ways we made practical use of these concepts.

Discovering Concepts, Inventing a Language   [150–167]

Synne: Maybe we can start with a question that Jamie McCarthy asked
me when we were making the work – I think it was in our second
week. He asked me, "What is it that you and David do when you
talk, and what did you do before the project – before we came
to Brighton?" He was just curious about what we did together.
I thought, "What is it that we do?" and I said, "We talk about the
work. We try and give it some kind of... it's not shape, but we try
and work out what it is; we try and work out the possibilities;
we try and create a language – a shared language for what it is
we're doing." And he said, "Well that makes a lot of sense.
I guess what you're doing is you're creating a conceptual space."
I didn't have those words at hand, but when he said that,
I thought, "Yes. That is what we're doing – we're preparing the
ground and creating a space; a conceptual space."

David: I think those conversations were about trying to find a way of
understanding what was happening. We'd always be trying to figure out
what to do with all the stuff that was emerging and which stuff was
relevant and which stuff might not be. So yes, we were making a space,
a space in which we could try and understand something, and, through
understanding it, try to work out what to do with it.

In the first R&D you said that you didn't want to make
'a theatre piece'.

I didn't want anyone to come to the piece with any expectation
of what it might be. I presumed that an audience goes to see theatre
with a certain expectation of how that might work for them as an event,
so as it became clearer that the experience for the audience was going
to be something different, it also became important to manage people's
expectations, so that we were free to make our own exploration of
the light.

So it was not going to be a story *about* light, and I think that
immediately made it necessary to say, "OK, it's not a process
where we generate lots of scenes and moments and then
organise them into some kind of brilliant structure." We had
to start somewhere else and much of the early R&D was about
trying to work out what it is if it's not theatre.

When I was thinking about what I wanted to do I was really clear that it wouldn't be theatre in the usual sense. But what it would be was less clear because I had so many different ideas, and there was this ongoing question, "what are we going to call it?" You can't call something 'not a piece of theatre'. It has to be something, and I remember writing maybe six or seven different proposals – probably that many – all slightly re-articulating the same bunch of ideas. And then there was a particular proposal when I used the phrase 'visual poem', and something suddenly became clear, simply because of the discovery of the idea of a poem – a visual poem. I mean, what does that mean? It's a very ambiguous thing anyway – 'a visual poem' – but it seemed to mean something as an alternative to theatre, and so the idea of making a poem became really vital.

I think the search for a language was also about creating a shared frame of reference for what we were doing because it was a project in two parts, and the first part involved only me and the second part involved many more people. The first part was entirely about experience and sensation and feeling and intensity of encounters with the light. I didn't try to understand anything about it. I didn't need to explain it either, and when I did need to explain it I found it very difficult, and the fact is that it was the discovery of a language involving the word 'poem' that allowed me to explain something that I hadn't been able to explain even to myself. So we needed to search for this language in order to work together, because how else could I articulate anything about my experience to anybody else who was working on the project? It wasn't just an intellectual exercise. It was necessary.

There's a real theme there, isn't there, with language: making sense of it for yourself by finding the words that will enable you to present it to other people.

Absolutely. We were trying to find language that liberated something rather than language that pinned anything down. We didn't want a language that would suddenly make something too clear and concrete too soon: it felt like our search for a conceptual language was about finding a way of working which would allow us to carry on searching, rather than one that would stop us.

A language that liberates.

Yes. And that's why it was like creating space. Creating some
spaces. Not specific. You know, you can move around in space, can't you?
There's room to move.

**Can we talk about the concepts of weather and weather systems?
The relationship between weather and emotions was apparent
from the beginning, but those concepts really began to inform
our work after a conversation with Ruth Little and Cathy Turner.[1]
It felt like another productive and liberating way to think about
the work, and certainly became a guiding principle when devising.
Like poetry it prompted a different way of thinking about how
and why things were happening within the structure. For
example I remember when we worked on a scene with Laura,
and it occurred to me that there had to be a sudden shift in pace.
With the idea of weather, as it's so erratic, we found a reason for
the shift in pace. We had license to shift direction or to do
something that was quite unpredictable due to our guiding
principle. And so we were trying, in any way we could, to weave
that idea of the weather's mood into everything. It felt quite
liberating to think of a piece in terms of its *behaviour*, as though
it was a kind of living organism, not just a structure that
tells a story through language.**

[1] We are grateful
to Ruth Little for
sharing her ideas
on weather and
natural systems.

Talking about the weather really made sense in terms
of understanding the nature of experiencing that piece as well,
for us and for the audience, because the weather feels like a really
tangible and really concrete sort of metaphor. Everybody is so intimately
and emotionally connected to the weather. We feel it. During devising,
we didn't talk directly about the audience's experience, because I think it's
sort of impossible to talk about that – "What do we want the audience to
experience at this point?" – I mean it's impossible. I don't know. How can
I possibly know what an audience will experience at this point in this piece?
But thinking about that unpredictable, endlessly changing weather-like
shift of feeling and response: that definitely felt right. It's like we made a
system of doing and watching and responding and feeling and looking and
hearing. I find it a very beautiful metaphor. The music is raining over here

and that causes a ripple of turbulence through a performer's body and that causes an upswelling of pressure in somebody watching it. The way that those different things are connected, I think is an incredibly beautiful idea for what performance is, and for what it does.

The notion of natural systems resonated on a number of levels, also because the notions of 'moving landscapes' or 'living poems' often emerged organically from our often very extended improvisations.

Yes, absolutely. We'd had those conversations with Ruth and Cathy about natural systems and chaos and unpredictability and change, and the way I understood that was by thinking of the structure as a landscape. We set up improvisations many hundreds of times in the process and most times, I would say, something really interesting and usually good came out of them. It's kind of extraordinary, you know. The company were really, really good at improvising. Then we made that decision, "OK. This is really good. You're really good at this. So this is what the piece can be", but then when we tried to explore that something else happened, it suddenly felt too chaotic, and it didn't feel possible any more, or it didn't feel like in the time we had it could be possible. There's something about looking at a natural landscape and all the different elements within it which are all completely disconnected and all operating in their own systems, and yet also of course completely connected by my eye, as the observer, and somehow influencing each other. But those things are not aware of being part of the picture that I'm looking at. But of course, performers completely are. We wanted the performers to behave like a landscape. It somehow made sense because there's an observer looking at them. But they knew that there was an observer looking at them and so the concept couldn't transfer into the reality of performance. And that was difficult, because it felt like the idea of a piece being like a landscape was again such a beautiful metaphor and so appropriate for this piece given what it was about.

So there's something about the transition from conceptual discussions and all these ideas, and then suddenly we're confronted with, "And so how does that work in the space?"

Yes, "How do you actually do that?"

"How does that feel for the performer?" or, "How do you construct that?" That becomes a very careful process, doesn't it? When we discovered that improvisation was not the way to go it became about meticulous composition, and you as a director had to somehow paint the landscape. But to create or understand the conceptual space and then for that to become reality, those are two different things.

Very different. So it felt in the end like the performance wasn't this incredibly open, fluid, ambiguous thing. Actually, it was a series of incredibly precise, directed moments and events and images and actions and sounds which, together, coalesced to make something that from an audience's point of view, yes, could very easily become ambiguous and fluid. But there was something about precision in our devising process and structuring process, about trying to get closer and closer to something in precise steps.

So in terms of the actual working process it seems a good idea to continuously address the *how* when discussing the *what* or *why*. So for example to address the practical ramifications for the working process when we develop a conceptual space, and to address what the process *needs*. "What practical and concrete things do these ideas need us to do?"

It's like there's a set of questions. And in a way answering those questions could be a whole ongoing project in its own right, you know, simply answering those questions, and I think we said to ourselves, "Here's one possible answer," and then we make this thing called *An Infinite Line: Brighton* and then we look at it and go, "Does this answer those questions? Is this a landscape or a weather system or a poem?" It's really difficult to answer those big conceptual questions, and to make a public piece, in the same process at the same time. I think that language was always most useful just to help us talk to each other about what was going on, and to give a kind of a framework, but I don't necessarily think that we were held back by it.

So there's this thing – whatever it is – over here in the performance. Is it in the performance because it somehow articulates the concept? No, it's not. It's in the performance because I love it and I want it to be there, because we love it. There's just something about it which feels important for a different reason, to do with something else, because again it felt like this space – this conceptual space that we made – was a space that we could move around in and it was fluid, so it never felt like it became an absolute limit on imagination or on possibilities.

Did those concepts help you when you were directing? Did it help you when you had to make decisions or when you had to think, "What's next? What is this landscape?" or, "Why is it there? Of course, it's the weather." Did it help you when you had to make decisions?

Yes, sometimes. The ideas we discussed around poetry were really helpful, often because it felt like they gave me a kind of permission to follow my instinct, actually, just to make a decision about something that I couldn't articulate to you or to the performers even, or to anybody else. We talked about poems being a language that doesn't explain itself or doesn't describe something, but rather a language that creates something. The landscape ideas and the metaphor of the piece as a kind of landscape – in the end I thought it was incredibly difficult. That was very different. That felt like a really difficult idea which we were trying to make real in some way, and I'm not sure that we succeeded. Sometimes, the landscape – the metaphor – sometimes it felt again like it was a kind of permission, because landscapes are complex and they demand a certain kind of attention from the viewer in order for them to make sense. They're not linear. Multiple things happen in them, you know. But then, on the other hand, a landscape's such a massively complex system, it felt like a really stupid thing to choose as a kind of guiding principle. My God! I mean, how do you make something like that? But in the end it's about questioning a way of looking, or of experiencing something, or questioning your way of working: it's a way to find new ways in, new ways to cause something to happen.

I remember something that Ruth said about natural systems – they can't be directed. You can't direct the weather. You can't direct the tides or the climate, but you can disturb them. I thought that was really interesting because it was also about language. You can't direct but you can disturb, and it's quite a thing as a director. What does that mean? In a rehearsal process, I don't direct, I disturb. I introduce disturbance into this – this system. I think I found that really useful.

But for example, that idea of disturbance: that actually happened, once the structure was in place, you did become the disturber because the performers took over. It became their piece and in the second week of the run you started to prompt and ask them and say, "OK, so what could happen here?" It became their piece and you took a step back in some way, whilst still making changes all the time, and so there was a whole new phase.

I think that's a very usual sort of directorial approach, isn't it? Not to actually direct, as in give an instruction to do something, but to question: "OK – what happens if you do this and you do that, and what happens if you try that? Is there anything in this idea? Can we look at this like that?" Just the fact of directing through the asking of questions does feel more like a kind of a disturbance rather than a direction, because you know it leaves a big space open and lots of different possible answers open up – answers to the question, whatever it is.

And the arrival of the audience. Really, the biggest disturbance of all. You know, the arrival of seventy or eighty people in our previously private space, every night. It's incredible what happens in terms of clarity in that moment, and that – yes, that disturbing force of an audience coming into a project. Yes, I think you're absolutely right. You enter a completely new phase and a different kind of territory, and you see things suddenly very differently and very clearly because you're in a room with all these other people who are having this experience for the first time. How incredibly clear things become by being part of that encounter.

What interested me a lot was the thing about ownership because we have this whole conceptual landscape or space that we'd created, and you talked to the performers and other collaborators about what it was, and you'd ask them questions to try to move them towards it. I remember Jamie Bradley saying something that was his way of articulating something you'd said, and I thought he'd found a wonderfully simple translation, at the same time as thinking, "Oh, yes, but it's *so much* more than that." But actually – no. He could stay with that thought, because that was his journey, and it was brilliant to think of it like that because we're talking about what it liberated for Jamie, what it is that liberates it for the performer to create the work, and his was a very simple and really good translation. I'm always curious as to how performers translate these very complex ideas into a very simple premise, because it has to be very simple, especially when you're working so much with improvisation, as we were.

It's about distillation. It's about the simplest way of understanding the essence of something. There were so many times when Laura or Jamie would say, "I've got no idea what this is, and I've got no idea what this looks like, or whether what I'm doing works, or if it's good", because they were there inside this picture which we'd created or inside this space which we were working in and we were somewhere else, looking in on them. So yes, that's absolutely right. All Jamie needs to think about is the clearly distilled idea he's found in some other, bigger set of concepts. Out here, looking in, there actually is something much more complex going on because we can see things from that different point of view. That's fine, and it's important that I might have one particular language, which you might articulate in a slightly different way, and which a performer might articulate in a slightly different way, and we'll all distil it to our own needs, and our needs are different. That's fine. I think we really needed to search together for a language or a frame of reference for what we were doing, because it was always necessary for the long conceptual conversations to turn into something functional and tangible and simple when it came to devising and improvising.

And there's something – you were talking about a kind of process of discovering something and devising, you know, and how something at some particular moment suddenly happens. Like the moment when Laura first improvised the thing we called the 'Roedean dance'. It grew out of all the work we'd been doing on movement and colour. But we hadn't spent all that time working towards that specific moment. That moment just suddenly happened. The possibility for something to happen suddenly was there in the space and we recognised the possibility. We recognised it and we recognised that we had discovered the key to the whole piece. Talking about weather and how things occur in a weather system and how something will emerge: suddenly there'll be an occurrence and that will cause something else to change. Suddenly there'll be a storm happening and that will cause something over there to do something different and that feels like a very potent or very important image for what a devising process is like: actually how important it is to be open and to be sensitive to those things which are emerging, or those opportunities for emergence which are presenting themselves. The work of a director in a devising process often feels like simply being attentive to the potential of what might be about to happen, or creating the possibility for something to happen, creating space for that possibility. It's not about focusing on what you think will happen or what you want to make happen. It's just keeping this constant sense of disturbance so that things might emerge.

> **It feels often when you devise that you're constantly preparing the ground for something. You're building a scaffolding. You're building a structure. It's like, "OK, let's just build this structure and keep doing things just knowing that at some point this theme will or must reveal itself and then we can build everything else around it, we can build our house around it." But it can be really frustrating because you often discover it quite late, and then you're in a real rush to get everything else working in the way you know it needs to work because you suddenly know what the piece is.**

It's a source of reassurance and a source of great terror to know that in a way it's already there. It already exists – the potential already exists. The thing will reveal itself. All I have to do is to notice it when it happens. I find that thought really reassuring, and really terrifying. If I know it's there I can trust that I will see it when it appears, but I have no idea when it's going to appear – and actually, what if I miss it? But then that's what it is isn't it? To be an artist of any kind, not just one using a devising process, but I imagine one of any kind: a sense of confidence that there is something, but an absolute knowledge that you don't know what it is.

> **I think what you're also talking about is finding an emotional content, and that was in a way what it was always about. I think for me that's another reason why the weather was potent, because I could connect with that as an emotional content.**

Yes. I think you're really right to talk about feeling and emotion as another kind of guiding principle, because it's very clear to me that in creating this conceptual space, and having discovered a language for talking about ideas (or a language for framing an experiment or improvisation, or as a way of posing a question that might lead to some material), we didn't use it strictly, it wasn't the only guide. You know, the R&D experiments led to a lot of really interesting and valid material that absolutely grew from the ideas and concepts and questions we were working with, but actually I often didn't like it. But I could very easily go, "Conceptually, this material is brilliant but in this piece and for me and to my taste and how I feel, it's not going to go any further." Remembering that feels really vital: that the conceptual wasn't separate from the experiential or the emotional.

The whole purpose is to find that one moment, and to see it and to feel it when it arrives, and so everything is a means to that end, in a sense, and everything brings it a step closer. And when that moment happens and you've had all this language and these discussions, you sort of don't need to talk about it because it becomes very clear what needs to happen. The conceptual discussions stop. For me the whole journey is actually not about concepts. It's not about those things as such. You don't even need to keep going on about why you're making the decisions. It becomes felt as much as thought.

There's something about intuition and a search for a different basis on which to make decisions that makes me think of poetry again. A poem doesn't try to explain something in the most straightforward, efficient or comprehensible way. It has to get beyond the surface of something to try and explain or reveal or allow the creation of something else, which is perhaps more hidden. There's also something really important about time and thinking about how poems operate in time, and the kind of time it takes to read a poem, and how slow you have to read. The connection between the temporality of reading a poem and the temporality of performance, and how you have this experience of watching and feeling something as a temporal event.

We talked at great length about how to invite the audience to slow down and stay with an image. Poetry asks a lot of you as a reader, I think, and maybe that's why the idea of poetry was so useful, because it helped us understand what this strange experience

was that we were making for an audience. It's important to remember that all of these ideas were informed, if you like, by the subject matter. The subject matter demanded a different approach. It wasn't just an idea that you suddenly thought of – "Oh, poetry!" Of course not: it started with the realisation that we were dealing with something that demanded a particular kind of language, something that demanded a particular kind of structure; actually something that demanded a very different conceptual space, and we needed to work out what that was.

But you know, ideas from poetry were useful on a really practical level too, sometimes. For example, in terms of a poem, there's this thing about rhyming, trying to see how you can create rhymes in a performance, and that was useful actually in terms of structure, I mean on the simplest level. There was an image of Laura, spinning this enormous mirror ball, making a spherical object turn in a circle, and then over there behind her is Jamie Bradley making a sound by moving his finger round the top of a wine glass. So she's down here turning this in a circle; he's up there turning that in a circle, and so these two things rhyme with each other on a visual level, and then she leaves this mirror ball and goes over there and picks up this transparent sphere and she starts to spin around and around with it as though she's trying to capture the atmosphere in it and, meanwhile, he's still up there with his finger going round the wine glass...

That's interesting.

...and, you know, the music is looping around them, another circle. I mean, that particular moment might have been the only point when that happened, but why were those three things happening at that point? Because I thought, "Ooh! What happens if I try and rhyme something with this image? Let's see what we can put together." It was useful. That said, in the end it wasn't really about the formal aspects of a poem – it was more about asking, "What does a poem do?" A poem makes something strange. It de-familiarises; it re-invents something; it's kind of radical because it, you know, yes, it re-imagines the world in a different way.

Yes. It invites the reader to re-imagine. It transforms. It's about creating a structure that is consciously trying to upset the rational

movement through it, because the experience itself isn't rational.

You know, the notes from the research visits – what was the purpose of the notes? I wrote them so that I would remember what I'd seen. Simply that – a simple aid to remembering, and I wrote them because I wanted to try and describe what I could see. When what you're trying to see is as indescribable and intangible as light, that puts such pressure on language that actually what I had intended to be absolutely a documentary piece of writing was forced towards poetry. It is exactly the same as we were trying to do in the performance. The performance wasn't about showing people what was out there in Brighton; it wasn't about, "Here is a set of images to describe something." It was absolutely about, "Here is a set of images and sounds and events and things in the space that might push you, the viewer, and push us, the people doing these things, through experience into something else." And through that transition – what do we want to happen? "We want you to leave this space and to encounter the light and the city and the world in a different way."

I think that's a really crucial point. I think it comes back to what we talked about before, that you didn't set out to create something called 'a visual poem' just for the sake of it. It was actually about the subject matter pushing you in that direction. The subject matter really pushed us in the direction of poetry – poetry, weather, landscape. I think that's a really important point, that you find the concepts that are appropriate to the topic itself, rather than the other way around. You're not imposing concepts onto it.

Yes, and like everything else that we've talked about, it was unexpected. It was unpredictable. That was the character of the whole project, wasn't it? We'd start out thinking, "Ah, we're going to do this," and then, "Actually, no. It's about this," or, "We're going to make a piece which is all improvised. Oh! No we're not," or, "We're going to make a twenty-four-hour durational piece. Oh! No we're not. We're going to make this. Oh! No, we're going to do that."

And of course what we're doing now is also talking about how you and I worked together. Our creative relationship was a process of talking through chaos and change until a kind of understanding eventually emerged.

And actually it's also sometimes a way of checking, "Are you seeing this, too, in this way?"

Yes. It's just, "Do you understand what I'm talking about?"

And I think that was a big part of creating a conceptual space, wasn't it? How do we talk about this? How do we think about this? How can we imagine this? What is this thing?

Yes, without killing it – you know, talking it to death. Talking it into being, really, was what we were trying to do. Talking something into existence, but in ways that were meaningful to us and understandable to us, and useful to us, actually. Maybe that last thing more than anything else – something useful that we could do something with, not talking for the sake of talking: the need to create something we could do something with practically. I mean, at some point in the past there was absolutely nothing at all, and then at some point there was this thing that people came to see. This thing exists, it has happened. So – yes, absolutely, giving it that body, building it, and finding a way to do that, building a space in which that can happen, and finding a language for talking about it when it does.

That's what everything was about.

Dialogue recorded
Hackney, London
July 2009

… STRUCTURE

How did we build the structure of the performance?

Probably more than any other piece I've made, *An Infinite Line: Brighton* was a tricky thing to structure. Because of the way we devise, with an equal emphasis given to the creation of images, movement and action, sound and music, light, space and design, and text, it's very easy to generate a large amount of material, but that material tends to be fragmented, episodic and impressionistic. This was compounded in this particular project because one of the central themes was change: how the light in Brighton was constantly shifting, endlessly new, always different. The light lacked a sort of constancy and through line, and we approached devising in the same way. As we've talked about elsewhere, we had an idea that the performance would be largely improvised, and only realised when we were well into rehearsals that this could not be the case. We decided instead to select, edit and structure the enormous amount of fragmented material we had created over the nine months of R&D and devising. This section lays out some of the ways we sought out the structure and some of the practical devices we used to find it.

A Lot Of Talking

The big question in this sort of work is:

WHY?

Why choose this material over that?

Why put these things together?

Why do it in this way?

Why this structure?

Because there is no guiding narrative and no pre-determined start, journey, or resolution, everything seems possible. This is where talking, and remembering the themes and the guiding principles, becomes very important. We already knew that a central idea would be that

[169]

the performance was a series of attempts to find a way of responding to the light: so we looked for material that had the strongest sense of 'effort'. We had conceptual guides, things like poetry, landscape, weather. As an idea, 'poetry' was useful: in building up one section I wanted to think about how images rhyme – a crude interpretation of how a poem works, but useful nonetheless. We ended up with a whole cluster of images of things turning in circles, one circle echoing, rhyming, the next.

Invent Criteria & Apply Them (But Ignore Them When You Need To)

One thing that repeatedly happened through these conversations, especially those with Synne, was that rules and limitations would emerge, which were useful to have when trying to make a structural or editing decision. Even if eventually you decide to break the rule, its presence can provide a framework to help you look at something differently, or to try something that you might not otherwise have considered. We applied rules such as:

Intention: focus on material which foregrounds how the performers are involved in a task of making the performance;

Search for a specific experience: avoid the generalised;

Repeat and persist: the performance has to continue until we have said something about the light.

Throughout the R&D process I had been making notes of themes and ideas and observations, and each of these was also useful as a reference point in this final phase.

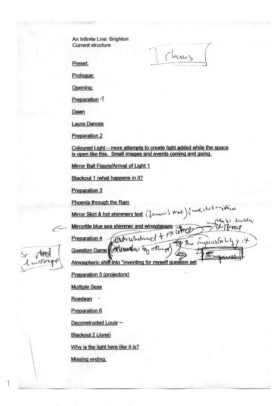

Imagined running orders:
Current structure,
Proposed new structure,
(Maybe) final structure

Infinite Line: Brighton
posed new structure

eset:

logue:

ening:

paration

wn

ra Dances

paration 2

oured Light – more attempts to create light added while the space
pen like this. Small images and events coming and going.

or Ball Figure/Arrival of Light 1 – bright silhouette making backlight

kout 1 (what is this? A lighting event? June description?)
6 mins

aration 3

enix through the Rain

or Skirt & hot shimmery text

ortile blue sea shimmer and wineglasses

aration 4

stion Game

ospheric shift into "inventing for myself" question set

r Ball Figure/Arrival of Light 2 – very bright backlight

kout 2 (how does this link to first blackout? Is it a direct repetition?
ting event? June description?)
mins

mosphere is created. A music improvisation, LC dances. JB
hes all – JB repeats instructions to them from a tape recording.
xt.

aration 5 (projectors)

An Infinite Line: Brighton
(Maybe) Final Structure

Preset

PART 1

Opening text into Wonderful World
Preparation 1
Dawn –check phoenix x entrance
Phoenix Arrives
Laura Dances in projection
Preparation 2, including Shadow game
Coloured Light
Laura tense text and new images – mirror tile bounce, cloud projection
which grows into
Mirror Ball/Globe/Arrival of Light 1
Blackout
Lights up – Jamie asks Laura what she's doing
Blackout (no blackout text from Laura going into this – costume change here)

PART 2

A Sexual Sound (used to be Multiple Seas, used to be at start of part 3)
Preparation 3
Phoenix through the Rain
Mirror Skirt
Laura walking on reflection and Jamie hot shimmery text
Mirrortile blue sea shimmer and wineglasses
Preparation 4
Question Game
Atmospheric shift into "inventing for myself" question set
Mirror Ball Figure/Globe/Arrival of Light 2 - Jamie speaks into the wind
Blackout 2

Part 3 →

Preparation 5 (projections – a very very slow reconfiguration)
Roedean
Why is the light here like it is? As Laura recovers
Wonderful world and very bright backlight. Everyone still. Phoenix. Silhouettes.
A long period of stillness and silence after the song.
Blackout

Major changes:

End of part 1 (mirrorball etc) builds to a climax, then snap to blackout
Jamie's "what are you doing" comes after this blackout, then there is a second
blackout here
Laura's "close your eyes" is cut
"Multiple Seas" has moved to the very start of Part 2, before the set change, and is
now called "A Sexual Sound"
Jamie B speaks into the wind machine at the end of Part 2
Part three starts with Roedean, with a tiny bit of new text tagged on the end

P.T.O →

Make Lists

When we began to search for a structure
I went back through all my notebooks
(there are four of them) and made lists
of all the things we had done during the
earlier stages of the project:

> Things from the August 07 R&D
>
> Sound and Music Discoveries
>
> Movements, Images, Events
>
> Elements from the Text R&D

Seeing all the material written out like
this was useful as a form of reassurance
(surely we would find a piece when we
had so much to work with) and a kind
of horror (what am I going to do with all
this?), but it was important that we didn't
overlook any of the things that we had
discovered much earlier in the process.

When trying to discover the structure,
I spent some time writing out an
imagined running order, a sort of live
list, in order to embed some patterns
and repetitions in what was starting
to feel like a structureless process.
This was altered and updated several
times (fig. 1). As an exercise, this was
very useful, providing another kind of
reassurance that something was
beginning to emerge, even though in
the end none of these was the actual
structure that we followed.

A Card For Each Thing

We had made so much material that I couldn't contain all of it in my head, so we spent an hour one day writing down everything that each of us remembered, everything that we liked. Each individual thing went onto a different notecard. We ended up with 69 cards. First we took out all the duplicates (we observed that the strongest material was that which all or most of us had written on our cards. This was reassuring – that we had so many common likes). Then we started to sort it into different orders of material, and added a note to each card to indicate the category, marked with a highlighter so we could identify them quickly:

text, movement, image, frames, music, chalk, light, season or atmosphere, projections

I made another category which comprised rejected material – things that I no longer wanted to work with.

Take Control Of Chaos

I also collated all the fragments of text that we had been working with, and stapled these together as a long fold-out strip. All the other texts were put away somewhere so that there were fewer things to consider. The staples simply stopped things getting lost in the mess of a working rehearsal room, as I knew I couldn't remember what had been there so wouldn't necessarily realise if something had gone.

Try, Take Note, Change, Try Again

Once we had the cards a process started to emerge through which I could see possibilities in the structure.

At the front of the space I had a table, covered with the cards. The first experiments in structure simply involved finding something that might be a beginning, then finding what might come next, and what next, putting these cards together and running through that material. See how it feels. Move things around. Try it again. Inevitably the first explorations were rejected. One day I was convinced I had found the opening, the next day I moved the same image to half way through a different clustering of ideas, and it felt better in this new position. Search for a different opening.

A Working 'Script' Endlessly Annotated

To try to keep control of this change-filled process, I put together a sort of working script. Describing different sections in words, and using the titles from our notecards, I could easily add and change and move ideas about sound, about lighting, about transitions, and could hand write notes and questions on the printed document, to consider outside rehearsal time. This document was like a musical score, and one that I could annotate, recompose, edit and change (fig.2). It was a reassuringly solid and physically present manifest-ation of a whole set of fluid and fleeting possibilities.

JM and DL play, LC speaks over mic (learnt text): *LX Laur cliv 1*

> important that DL and JM are lit, not just LC.

5.45 am: Colours

A paling, brightening sky: from violet steel to now midgrey with barest blue behind. To the West: the sky deadsalmon pinkgrey, grey, pale blue. To the East: pale grey, pinkgrey bruise deadsalmon. The sea mercury: molten metal, silvergreen. The sea an indescribable cold molten silver green grey, a dull mirror, opaque, surface churns, bouncing back the brightening pale grey sky.

I think it's daytime now. The change is imperceptible and incredibly quick. Each time I look up; brighter. Where is the sun? ✱ — *→ PHOENIX ENTERS*

→ LX Laur cliv 2

End of text: frame end slides in behind LC. ~~She moves out of way as projection is turned on by JB.~~

> why does L move? This moment not clear. Blue dress brought to her, she changes. Very low light, the chair is struck. The projection comes on.

LX Laur chngs

Laura Dances

LX Blackout

Projection of sea on frame end. **LC changes into blue dress**, watching the projection. She starts to dance, moving closer to the image, finally enters it. She dances and her shadow dances, in the projection.

Reposition / Frame

DL plays the colour of the projection, JM plays the light.

Lights snap black to bright white, LC is caught in the moment of dancing. An awkward moment.

> what is this moment? Not clear. The relationship between JM and LC needs to come back. (What are you doing?)

feeling ly / w Literally

Preparation 2

LX Preparation 2
Add LX here

FX: "Dog Grumble", as set is rearranged.
JB goes behind back frame and frame is closed

Coloured Light

ECHO / SHADOW → or plays

JM is sitting far upstage. JM and MW play high tones together, the space dark.

> break down the sound more – just ~~MW~~ *JM* at first, then ~~JM~~ *MW* joins.

Changes LC s b

Strike of tape player after intro - to mid SL (c

LX JB cue to non-fiz light.
Wind machine into pre-blackout 1 ?
Not enough light for Jm questioning

COMB BACK TO LATER / CHAN

NOTES TO GIVE

DON'T FORGET

X
f
F
h
H
s
s
s

and which later were changed to tell me where in my increasingly illegible notes to find:

> things to come back to later and change

> notes to give

> things not to forget

As we clustered together notecards and copies of texts, I started to develop a system for making sense of how things might work together, or what needed to happen with each fragment for it to work with those around it *(fig.3) >*

INVISIBLE THINGS

1 This is the title we gave to this cluster of ideas.

2 I've no idea what W2.2 means. It must have meant something to me at the time.

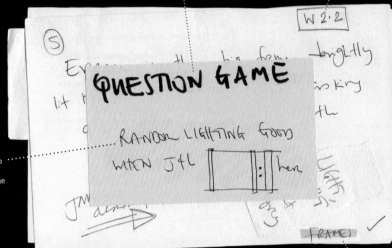

3 This is a note for myself to pass on to Billy, who was controlling a set of onstage fluorescent strip lights, which were randomly coming on and off during this section.

4 The blue highlighter pen is part of a colour coding system for making sense of the note cards. Blue means that this set of ideas is performance based.

5 This description is of something we discovered in the development workshops in August 2007. During the April 2008 rehearsals, we all wrote down the things from the research and development that we remembered and liked, and this is one of the ones I wrote. It is the beginning of the evolution of the Question Game.

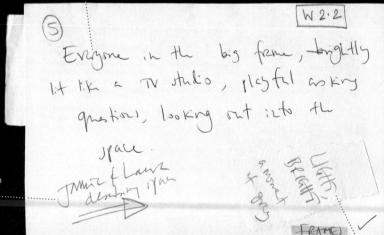

6 This is a note I scribbled on the card once it had developed beyond being a memory from the research period and started to become something specific we were doing in the performance.

7 *"LIGHT BRIGH!*
a moment of grey."
I have no idea.

response to the question *"How do I feel?"*
– the answer: *"Tired. Like I'm searching for something that I only find if I invent it for myself."* This line became fundamental to the performance, and was probably the most important thing anyone said in the show. It came to represent the idea that the whole project was an attempt to find something worth saying in response to that already-extraordinary light.

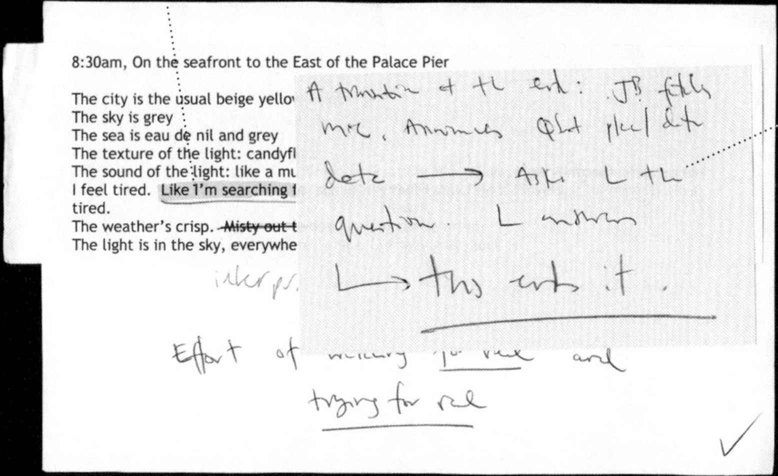

8:30am, On the seafront to the East of the Palace Pier

The city is the usual beige yellow
The sky is grey
The sea is eau de nil and grey
The texture of the light: candyfl
The sound of the light: like a mu
I feel tired. Like I'm searching f
tired.
The weather's crisp. ~~Misty out t~~
The light is in the sky, everywhe

[handwritten post-it note:] A mention of the end: JB fills mic, Announces что plce/ date date → Asks L the question. L answer L → this ents it.

interp.

Effort of ~~~~ for rel and trying for rel

9 This is a note about how this section ends, a note about structure that allowed me to tie this card and set of ideas into the ones that follow. The post-it note refers to the text that is beneath it.

10 This is a note to say that the most important thing about this section is that the effort of trying to find a way of describing the indescribable is a real effort. Not acted, never repeated, but always real.

11 This was a 'memory card' which Laura wrote out, which I connected with my own memory. She's remembered an improvisation from the movement workshops we did in London in January 2008, when I'd asked each person to express a colour or a weather through their body, and then asked the others to recreate it. It was really hard to do.

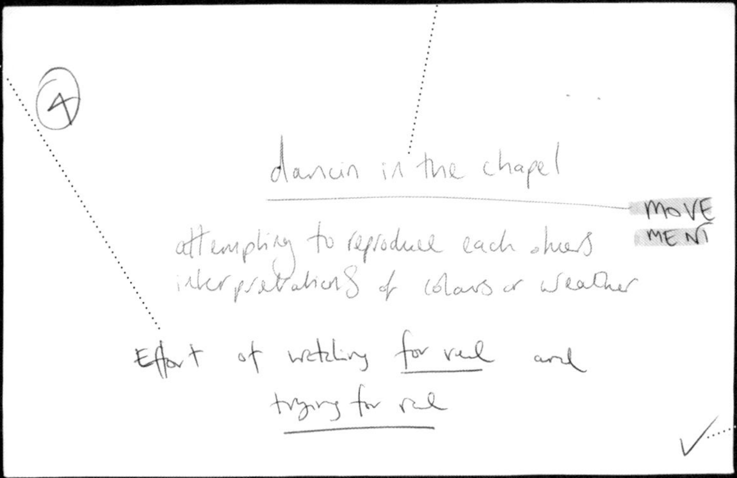

[handwritten, circled:] A

dancin in the chapel

MOVE MENT

attempting to reproduce each ones interpretations of colours or weather

Effort of watching for rel and trying for rel

12 The tick means that this set of images, movement words and ideas made it into the final edit. Tick!

3

Drawings And Illustrations

At the end of the final week of rehearsals, we still didn't have an ending. One night, I drew out a complex diagram of things that I thought might work together to make one. There was an idea that this final section would be very cluttered, very full, building to a sort of chaotic climax and then a sudden stop, feeling like a living landscape of material. *'Make a Landscape'* was my instruction to myself. The idea was a red herring: to build a chaotic structure is to not build a structure at all, but what it did reveal is that we had already pretty much found the ending, we just hadn't recognised it as such. Drawings and visualisations are useful though, as a way of bringing different possibilities together and keeping a handle on them: any visual tool, even if you quickly come to reject it, is a help.

Give Yourself A Break

This particular idea led to a day of drifting and unfocused improvisation which was really important after two weeks of exhaustingly intense structural explorations. We unfolded my map, *'Make a Landscape'*, and played with things within it. I stopped directing. I left David to improvise on his bass for most of the day; we set up a load of projections then let them run without knowing why. We ate a lot of biscuits. We stopped pushing. We retreated from the effort and from the insistence. I knew this wasn't moving us any closer to finding our ending, our structure, but I also knew that we simply needed to make an open space like this, to step back, to pause, to stop.

Useful Tools

I couldn't have done it without:

a set of highlighter pens;

a box of paper clips (to group things together, to help me realise that what I had thought were five different things could in fact be one thing);

a stapler ("Yes! these five things *are* one thing: there's a decision");

a Post-It pad (don't write directly on things when you might change your mind, write it on a note, later you can clip it, then you can staple it, or you can take it away again);

and a desk that no-one else was allowed to use (a small place of order and focus in the mess and madness of a cluttered creative space).

You're Not In This Alone

It's easy to lose sight of what things are working and what things are not. I find that as soon as my attention shifts from the creation of material to the structuring of it, I start to dislike things that I had previously loved. I'm aware of this self-sabotaging, and I have learned how to ignore it, but sometimes it's genuinely hard to know whether something is working, whether it's the material itself or your perception of it that's the problem.

Within the creative team, there were key people who I would work closely with to try to keep a clear perspective on the material:

Synne, of course, in the role of dramaturg;

[178]

Ali, who I trust to always be honest in her response to the material, and who knows me well enough to know what I'd be trying to achieve;

and Mark, who was always slightly outside the frame of the performance as he was creating material from an offstage sound desk.

This is also the point at which you could invite someone else to look at things with you, with fresh eyes – someone from outside this core team. It has to be someone you trust and it has to be someone who understands your work, who has a handle on what it is you do (there's no point inviting someone who expects to see a 'well made play' to look at material that is deliberately slow and drifting). Show them some stuff. Have a cup of tea, and a chat, and a good cry if you need it. See what they think.

Sam fulfilled this role, coming in once a week to have a look at what had been going on,

as did Louise, the project's producer.

If they affirm something you suspected, go with it, follow their advice. If they make you feel protective of what you were doing and you think they are wrong, trust that this means that you are right. At the end of the day you have to make something that *you* love. Other people's dislike can help you focus on what you like. These 'openings up' – within the creative team and to other people – helped move things on when we got stuck, bringing a new injection of energy and motivation to the process.

Follow Your Instinct First

I wanted to make initial structural decisions on my own (as when I drew together an initial sort of running order, a list of elements in the piece), and to only then open these up to discussion – with Synne, with the rest of the team, with these 'outside eyes'. On other projects, this initial sketching has been much more collaborative, and based in dialogue, but on this one, which was driven so much by an individual point of view, it was useful for something very concrete to appear as a starting point for other experiments and conversations and debates. It provided a place to start.

Be Realistic About What's Happening Here

Some of the decisions I made around structure were made for less than creative reasons. There were a lot of images that we had found with the movement of the set that simply couldn't work when we had to factor in the presence of a horse. We had always done lots of work with chalk and with water, but again these were problematic with a horse in the room (the floor became dangerously slippy), and stopped the set moving freely. When we had focused purely on sound and music we had made some brilliant discoveries, but in trying to blend these things with other material (image, text, movement) we simply couldn't find them a home. Although it was painful, we had to let them go.

Remember How Different Things Look When The Audience Arrives

In the end it was only when we were doing public performances that I really clearly began to get a sense of the possibilities of the material, to see and feel what was really working, and to realise where I had gone wrong. At this stage, we were able to make small changes to the detail but larger structural shifts were hard (we had no rehearsal time as the space was in use during the day with the installation). Something happens to perception when the energy of an audience meets the energy of the material, and through that meeting and that friction things often clarify. Although with this particular project the possibility for change was limited, it has shifted how we now plan our new work, always factoring in ongoing rehearsals and scheduling time and space in which the structure can continue to develop, and be clarified, and change.

At the end of a project, when everyone has left, when the space is quiet, when a landscape of light is overgrown by darkness, what remains?

Conclusion [182–191]

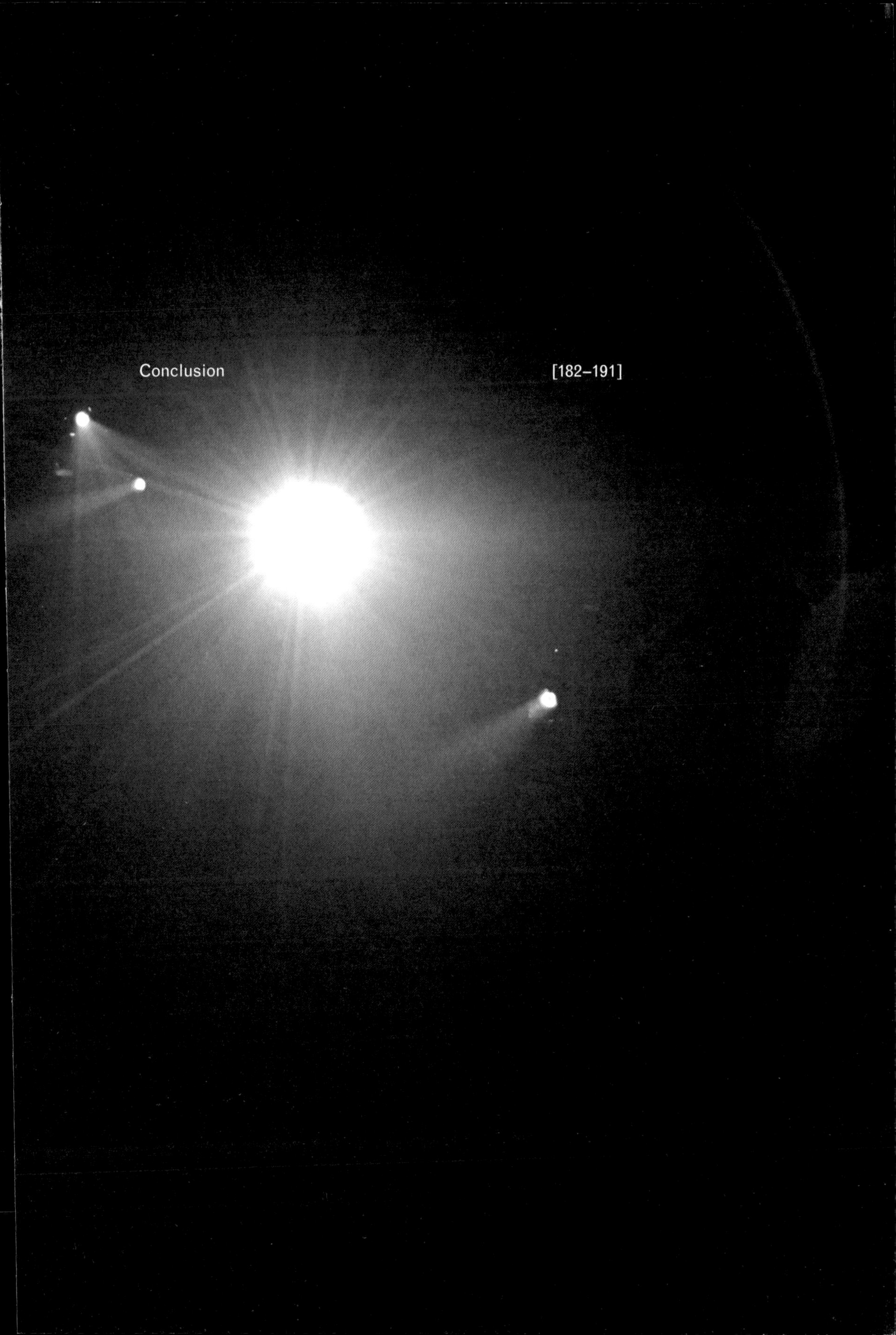

What remains?

(what colour is the city?)

I remember all the things we discovered in devising, all the things we talked about in the R&D. I remember all the images, all the sounds, all the moments when a small rip appeared in the fabric of the process and it was possible to see through to a time and a place when *it exists.*

(what colour is the sea?)

I remember blue and grey and pinkblue and greengrey and silver and gungrey and white.

(what colour is the sky?)

I remember what we made. And I remember what we lost.

Devising is a process in which the potential becomes the actual and the hidden becomes the present. It is also a process in which the material becomes the insubstantial and the visible becomes the invisible. Devising is a process of creation and it is a process of loss.

All the images, all the sounds, all the moments when something flared up briefly in the room: sometimes the camera blinked its mechanical eye to take a look and these things can still be seen. Sometimes there was no time to see before the moment had passed and these things slip through memory to a place of nonbeing. To a place of loss.

Devising is a process of creation and it
is a process of loss.

(what colour is the sky?

I can't remember.
It is changing too fast)

We ended up with so much material,
so many things, so many possibilities.
We ended with so much that was
incomplete, so many ideas still to
explore, so much still to do. Devising:
this project nothing more than a fast and
furious pause in an ongoing process,
a chain of questions strung out and left
unanswered, strung out in the light,
for the light, and some answered and
most unanswered. And some questions
remain, even now, even after: how do we
do this? How do I do this? How do I want
to do this? What process must I invent,
this time, in order to do this? Each
project a part of a body of work, a beacon
on a chain of lights strung out in the
darkness, some flickering on, some
brightly lit, some dark, some broken.

(where is the light, now?

On the garlanded beach-side
lights, cats' eyes, blinking, faint)

At the end of a project, when everyone
has left, when the space is quiet, when
a landscape of light is overgrown by
darkness, what remains?

A cloud just above the floor.

The silhouette of a horse.

A mirror ball.

A strip of colour.

A pair of headphones and a voice.

An exhausted body briefly turned
to light.

INVISIBLE THINGS

At the end of a project, when everyone has left, when the space is quiet, when a landscape of light is overgrown by darkness, what remains?

(how do I feel?

Like something has finally ended; like something is just about to begin)

Jamie rides a bicycle around the rehearsal room.

Laura's hands strobe in the flickering light.

The sound of the tide rises and falls.

Someone falls asleep in rehearsals.

A projector stutters and whirrs.

The light is out there in the street.

The damp dark smells of wet plaster and dust and dirt.

The line of the horizon is a dull metallic grey slicing apart the sea and the sky.

There is no conclusion to draw, nothing to sum up. We went there. Something happened. We made something happen.

And after, now that it's happened, now that it's gone, what remains?

I remember a seagull flying on a block of chalk.

A series of frames like a courtroom, like a trial.

Flickering sealight on the bricks of the wall.

Arms like wings, outstretched.

Fog.

I lift the lid of the box. Here is a bound set of notes, notes from a year of visits, to look at the light. Here is a muddle of paper, notes, words, mnemonics. Here is a disc of films, here is a disc of music, here is a disc of electronic sounds. Here, at the bottom of the box, is a folder. Here is everything, carded, notes to help us remember what we had done. Here is a bundle of cards, with a note. It says, 'Rejected Material':

Using the dust from the chalk to whiten Laura's face.

Chalk dropped by hand, and a projection of a seagull in flight on the dust.

A buried tape recorder.

Wires played like strings, bowed and processed, the sound of a wire becoming voice.

A procession of shadows and a microphone.

A voice made distant by a megaphone.

Repeating words as music.

A pattern repeated forever in every part of your body the same every time and different and in a different part of your body every time repeated forever.

Voices trapped in the loop machine.

Projections refracted through a wineglass to make a dance of water.

A catwalk polished for a metallic dress.

A curtain made of rain.

Everyone just very softly singing *What a Wonderful World*.

An attempt to speak through a storm.

A body jumps into a floodlight and disappears.

A globe full of water.

A horse moving fast through the whole clear space.

INVISIBLE THINGS

What remains?

What colour was it?	*A very smooth dark greybrown, flecked with sharp shards of brilliant colour.*
What colour is the memory?	*A faint red, still fading, but rich, but fading.*
What colour are these remains?	*Foil, Quality Street; pure white; the colours of the light about six feet beneath the surface of the sea; ashgrey.*
What do you hear, now?	*Something coming to a stop; a grinding, a breath, a sigh.*
What texture does it have?	*Very polished, smooth, sensual. It makes your mouth water, and it will slice clean through your hand.*
Where is the light, now?	*Very distant: a point just above the horizon. And everywhere, all around, making seeing anything else impossible.*
How do you feel?	*Tired, I feel tired. Like I've been searching for something I can only remember if I invent it for myself. Like I know so much about it, but I still can't be sure what it was.*
What's the weather like?	*The weather is turbulent. It's unpredictable. The weather will not be forecast. On a day when it's due to be dark and cold and flat and hard, the sun unexpectedly comes out, and something shines. On a day when it will be hot and clear it's oppressively close, too hard to think, to fugged to see. Today there is a fresh breeze and we can breathe and we can move again. Today the wind is too fierce and I can't hear anything else for the noise it makes. We can't speak to each other for the noise it makes.*
	(Re-read: the weather of devising is turbulent).

INVISIBLE THINGS

At the end of a project, when everyone
has left, when the space is quiet, when
a landscape of light is overgrown by
darkness, what remains?

Devising is a mechanism for losing
things and moving things and
shifting things and killing things;
for forgetting things and finding
things and loving things and choosing
things and showing things.

Devising is a map in which only some
of the landscape is visible.

Devising is landscape half submerged
beneath a violent sea.

Devising is what's washed up on a swell
of work and thought and inspiration.

Devising is having to get out of bed
and go to work when all you want to
do is sleep.

Devising is joy, and it's exhaustion,
and it's fear, and it's love.

Devising is a lot of coffee and a lot of
biscuits and a lot of tea.